LANTERN PRESS BOOKS

are complete and unabridged reprints of titles in the several series of thematic short-story anthologies published originally by Lantern Press, Inc. Over two million copies have been sold in their higher-priced, cloth-bound editions.

Teachers, librarians, and reviewers have often recommended these carefully edited anthologies. For instance, *Scholastic Teacher* said: "All are suitable as supplementary readers for junior high school students. Each title appears on most school and library approved reading lists and is recommended by *The Library Journal*. Though mainly for junior high school readers, they can be read with pleasure by older students and they are endorsed by Spache in GOOD READING FOR POOR READERS."

A complete list of the titles now available will be found on the reverse side of this page. If your bookseller doesn't have a title you want, you can get it by sending retail price, local sales tax if any, plus 35¢ per book for postage and handling to Mail Service Department, POCKET BOOKS, a Division of Simon & Schuster, Inc., 1 West 39th Street, New York, N.Y. 10018. If you are ordering for delivery in Canada, send retail price plus 35¢ per book for postage and handling to Simon & Schuster of Canada, Ltd., 330 Steelcase Road, Markham, Ontario. In either case, please send check or money order. We cannot be responsible for cash.

MORE
DOG
STORIES

Edited by
A. L. FURMAN

ORIGINAL TITLE: *Everygirls Dog Stories*

A LANTERN
PRESS BOOK

PUBLISHED BY POCKET BOOKS NEW YORK

MORE DOG STORIES
(Original title: *Everygirls Dog Stories*)

Lantern Press Book edition published May, 1966

5th printing .... July, 1976

"It Shouldn't Happen to a Dog," Copyright, 1950, by NEA Service Inc., reprinted by permission of Lee Priestley; "The Sensational Type," Copyright, 1950, by Triangle Publications for *Seventeen*; "Love Me, Love My Dog," Copyright, 1962, by The Methodist Publishing House, reprinted from *Twelve/ Fifteen*; "Dog Gone," Copyright, 1951, by Boy Scouts of America, reprinted from *Boys Life* Magazine by permission of Anne Hall Smith; "Pinafore for Pam," Copyright, 1954, by The Methodist Publishing House, reprinted from *Twelve/ Fifteen*; "The Prize Ticket," Copyright, 1945, by *Seventeen*, used by permission of Ann Napier.

This POCKET BOOK edition includes every word contained in the original, higher-priced edition. It is printed from brand-new plates made from completely reset, clear, easy-to-read type.
POCKET BOOK editions are published by
POCKET BOOKS,
a division of Simon & Schuster, Inc.,
A GULF+WESTERN COMPANY
630 Fifth Avenue,
New York, N.Y. 10020.
Trademarks registered in the United States
and other countries.

ISBN: 0-671-68014-5.
This Lantern Press Book edition is published by arrangement with Lantern Press, Inc. Copyright, ©, 1963, by A. L. Furman. All rights reserved. This book, or portions thereof, may not be reproduced by any means without permission of the original publisher: Lantern Press, Inc., 354 Hussey Rd.,
Mt. Vernon, N.Y. 10552.
Printed in the U.S.A.

Contents

More Dog Stories

Botch Dog

CARL HENRY RATHJEN

THE botch dog began barking at 9:35 that night when his cocked ears painfully caught the shrilling sirens before Beth Sanders heard them.

"Sarge! Quiet!" she pleaded, thinking he was just pestering her for a walk, the same as all evening while she tried to cram for high school final exams.

Sarge, part blue-black shepherd with tan under-markings of some vagrant Doberman ancestry, obeyed by going to the partly open window. He whined, piped, then came back to Beth and nudged her arm with his cold nose.

"Oh, be a good dog for once," she said absently, trying to keep weary eyes focused on the solid geometry text. Why did she have to waste time with that subject anyway? She wasn't going to need it when she became old enough to follow the career which made most of her girl friends raise their eyebrows. She wanted to become a police woman, and maybe if she made it the Department would let her have her dead father's shield. But in all he had taught her about people, laws, and taking care of herself he had never once mentioned the need for solid geometry. Neither had Mel Weber, who was already on the force, and who said that he had other ideas about a career for her.

Beth sighed. Well, she needed the high school diploma before she could apply to the police department, and to get the diploma she had to get solid geometry. So, gritting her teeth, she concentrated again on the theorems and corollaries.

Then Sarge vociferously pulled out all the stops. His clamor shattered cubes, cylinders, and prisms.

"Quiet!" Beth raged impatiently. "You'll wake up Billy and Kathy. Do you want the muzzle?"

Sarge's brown eyes gave her a sad, don't-do-that-to-me-pal look. Then Beth heard the sirens too. They never gave her a scary feeling, not even at night. They always meant that someone like Mel was on the way to help someone else. And maybe some day she'd be part of what they meant. But Sarge didn't like them and he was letting her know loudly, making her ears hurt too.

"Sarge!" she commanded sternly. "The neighbors will call you a nuisance again! A watch dog who's become a botch dog! Always barking at the wrong things! Always—"

"Beth," her mother chided from the door behind her. "You make more noise than he does."

"This Beanbrain rattles my brains," said Beth, but at the same time she gently placed her hand on his muzzle and closed her fingers lightly about his jaw.

10

"It's time you quit anyway," Mrs. Sanders said. "If you don't know your geometry by now you won't know it in the morning." A twinkle appeared in her soft gray eyes. "Besides, Sarge has been very patient, waiting for his w-a-l-k."

That broke up the cram session. It never failed. The big botch knew how to spell. He went into berserk circles, tail banging Beth and every piece of furniture in the den. He raced out, ridged the hall runner with a sliding stop, slammed back into the den, knocked over the waste basket, leaped up with paws creasing the pages of the geometry book. His eager barking failed to drown out the sirens which were coming closer.

Beth saw her mother's eyes become misty.

"They always remind me of your father," she murmured. "He would have liked Sarge. But I don't think even he could have made Sarge like sirens."

She smiled at Sarge's antics as he raced out to the kitchen where his leash hung, then charged back to the den to urge Beth to hurry. Beth got wearily to her feet.

"Maybe it's more our fault than Sarge's," she admitted.

Sarge had been a birthday gift from Mel two years ago, soon after her father died in a crash while pursuing a hit-and-run driver. Mel had advised her to be stern in the pup's upbringing. But instead of making Sarge into a worthy watch dog, Beth had joined her family in pampering, petting, and producing a too friendly pooch. A botch dog. Whenever a stranger rang the doorbell, Sarge raced

11

to the door with welcoming, not warning, barks. He'd probably lead any burglar to the silverware. And he went against all canine instincts by loving cats! But his appearance did hold strangers at a distance, until they got onto him. Anyway, he was a pretty good, though demanding, pal.

So Beth got the leash; or rather, Sarge led, hazed, and jawed her to it. Then, with the slack of it in his teeth, he dragged her to the front door and down the front steps, all three of them in one jump. Beth tightened the leash to remind him who was boss of this expedition. He yanked her onto the lawn beside the camellias.

Beth turned her head to listen to the sirens. Some of them died out about three blocks away, up on Main Street. But another still sounded, coming from the east, and far down her street she saw the flashing red light of a police car or an ambulance coming from the south. She wondered what was going on up on Main Street. A bad accident or what?

Sarge interrupted her surmises by hauling her down to the maple at the curb to see who had registered in the neighborhood while the evening was wasted with geometry. The cool night air soothed Beth's weariness. She took deep breaths to help clear her muddled brain.

Across the way she could see the bluish-white glow of the TV screen in Haskells'. She could even hear the voices, the drumming hooves, the gunshots. The Haskells were a childless, petless couple who lovingly manicured their lawn, frequently

12

complained about Sarge's barking, but thought there was nothing wrong in turning up the volume of their TV. And the Butlers next door to Beth also complained about Sarge, but let their cat Calico a loose all night to yowl.

Beth could have got into plenty of arguments with the neighbors, but she always remembered that her father, in teaching her judo and karate, had also told her that control of the tongue muscles was important too in dealing with people. So, perhaps too often, Sarge served as a safety valve for annoyances; but he was a pretty good sport about it.

Beth hauled him away from the maple. "Come on, Goof, this is supposed to be a walk."

Then the police car came up the street with its spotlight slashing the night from side to side. It slowed, focusing on Beth with a blinding glare, then angled rapidly across toward her. It was a new model car, so Sarge couldn't have recognized it by engine sound. He'd been busy at the tree, and now the glare prevented his seeing the red flasher on the turret top. So to all intents, this car could have been full of hold-up men, abductors, some kind of trouble for Beth. But all her protector did was wag his tail, eagerly lift his head and cock his ears while he made friendly piping whines. Cooing would have been a better way to express it.

The spotlight snapped off, and Mel's voice came from the darkness.

"Don't let him claw the car, Beth, or slobber all over me."

Beth laughed, holding Sarge back. "That's a nice

13

way to to talk about your gift to me. Thanks for warning me. You know the old saying. 'Love me, love my dog.' "

"He's too loving," Mel said dryly. As Beth's eyes adjusted she saw his grin. But it wasn't as relaxed as usual, and there was a glint in his eye she'd often seen in her father's when he'd been on a tough case or called out on special duty. "I am warning you, Beth. Get in the house and don't open the door for anyone. But first, have you seen a stranger around here? A man on foot?"

Beth became more aware of the night chill. "I just came out," she replied. "What's up?"

Beyond Mel, his partner whom she didn't recognize started to answer. "There's been—"

"Uh-uh!" Mel cautioned. "Don't give her any ideas. This gal," he added with a touch of reluctant admiration, "would try to do a policeman's work. Beth, please don't insist or argue. Just get in the house and don't open the door for any strangers."

As a policeman's daughter, Beth knew when to take orders.

"All right," she promised. "As soon as I can drag Sarge in."

"Boot him in," Mel said kindly, then the police car went on with its spotlight probing side to side.

The night was suddenly very dark, the neighborhood deserted. A falling maple leaf made its noisy, labyrinth way down through the tree. Beth hunched instinctively, then let Sarge pull her to the far edge of a street light's sallow aura. But no farther, not when there were shadows her eyes couldn't penetrate, not when she'd promised Mel.

Shortening Sarge's leash, she forced him back on the lawn toward the house. He could nose around in the fenced yard tonight. He always insisted on it anyway, no matter how long a walk he'd been on. Besides, Beth wanted to get a newscast on the radio, or tune in the police band and find out what was going on. It was far more exciting and interesting than solid geometry.

Sarge detoured her from the front steps to the thick evergreens beside the house. Leaning on his leash, he gave that piping whine again. Beth knew what that was about. The Butlers' calico cat liked to crouch under that bush every night. Usually after everyone was in bed. Then he'd loudly settle scores with other neighborhood Toms. He hadn't yet learned that Sarge was canineless as far as felines were concerned, and Beth never tried to correct that misconception. She gave Sarge plenty of slack for a loving lunge. Calico always misconstrued it for ferocity; would give a spitting hiss and make a tunnel through the night while Beth took a few running steps with Sarge in pursuit to keep up the deception.

Tonight, it went as per formula. The lunge. The hiss. But that was all. Because it wasn't Calico in the darkness of the bushes. It was a man in a plaid shirt that looked like calico in the dark.

"Hold it!" he hissed. "Keep your mouth shut and that mutt back or I'll let you both have it!"

Beth turned to stone, still cold from the Ice

Age. She remembered how Sarge had whined at the window of her den, trying to tell her someone was out there. Now her watch dog leaned on his leash and showed his teeth—in a grin—wagged his tail and whined. The botch!

"Hold that mutt short," warned Mr. Calico. He stepped out from behind the bush. His towhead was tousled. His eyes as cold and glinting as the gun. He studied the street behind Beth, but he never stopped watching her too. "We'll go inside," he said. Sarge piped eagerly.

Beth stood rigid, thinking of her mother, Billy, and Kathy. And she was also thinking of herself. Her stomach was putting the squeeze on her. It didn't want to digest any lead. She was also recalling how Mel taught judo and karate, how to cope with a gun or a knife. But it was one thing to have a practice session with an unloaded gun in a friendly hand. It was something else now to stare at that little black hole in the faint glow from the street light. It could all be summed up in one word. Period.

Mr. Calico motioned commandingly. Beth moved slowly toward the front steps. If she found the nerve to try anything, Sarge was too much of a handicap rather than a helper. She had to drag him because he was trying to be Mr. Calico's dog instead of hers. She was tempted to release him, so that he would be a handicap to Mr. Calico, but he would undoubtedly also be shot. She dragged him to the steps and suddenly felt as though she'd put on too much weight for her legs.

16

On the porch she paused while Sarge did a happy tap dance with his claws and a hula tail-wag. Mr. Calico kept his distance. He nodded his towhead toward the door.

"Open it."

Beth found her voice. "I forgot my keys," she lied, and knew—as she had always told her little brother and sister—you have to pay for it when you lie. She and her mother had a pact. If either one of them were on the porch with a stranger, the other would not open the door until certain that everything was all right, no matter what the one outside said. That way, only one of the family would be harmed if the stranger didn't take to flight. The others would be safe in the locked house and able to summon help.

Mr. Calico looked at Beth threateningly.

"No keys," Beth repeated. "I'll have to ring the bell . . . but I won't." She surprised herself by suddenly moving to block the bell button so he couldn't get to it without coming near Sarge. Her voice trembled. "You can shoot me . . . or the dog . . . but what good is that going to do you? The whole neighborhood will be aroused."

Mr. Calico laughed silently. "Why should I do anything like that, Sis, when your mother is opening the door for us?"

Beth whipped a startled glance over her shoulder. Her mother couldn't see Mr. Calico standing to one side. She must have thought everything was all right because Sarge, the family protector, wasn't giving her any reason to think otherwise. The botch dog stood looking up at the stranger, and at the same time his wagging tail was thumping the door's lower panel, the way he always knocked when he wanted in or out!

Before Beth could scream a warning, her mother opened the door. Sarge surged into the opening, so there was no chance to yank the door shut. Mr. Calico shoved Beth, and Sarge pulled her in. Beth's mother stepped back under the menace of the gun. Mr. Calico closed the door with his shoulder. Sarge turned, giving a happy greeting whine, sitting very erect with his tail going like a windshield wiper on the floor.

"Thanks, pal," Mr. Calico said to him. "I'm glad I didn't put a new part in your skull."

He lowered his left hand, palm up. Sarge sniffed the fingers, then licked them. Beth gave her mother a long look—a split-second can be long at a time like that.

"Careful, Sis," said Mr. Calico. "Thinking can be very risky." He shot a glance out at the deserted street. "Let's get away from these windows."

The wiring from Beth's brain to muscles met resistance somewhere, but again Sarge helped her obey. To him, company always meant something to eat. Hand-outs. It was another point where she'd failed in his stern, watch-doggy upbringing. Tugging so hard he wheezed on his leash, he pulled her through the dark dining room into the kitchen where the shades were drawn.

"Who else is home?" Mr. Calico inquired.

Mrs. Sanders started to shake her head.

18

"My brother and sister," Beth replied. "They're only seven and five. They're asleep."

For a moment her mother looked horrified. Then she must have realized Beth's way was best. If one of the children came walking out sleepily, and unexpectedly, and this trigger-happy man didn't know they were in the house . . .

"That's the entire family," Mrs. Sanders said curtly. "And there's very little jewelry or cash in the house."

Mr. Calico's gun motioned Beth toward the breakfast nook.

"In the corner, Sis. Keep the pooch on the leash with you. Now relax, you've had a hard evening of homework. I saw you through the window before you came out."

"A peeping Tom!" Mrs. Sanders snapped. "If you think—"

As a policeman's wife, who'd been trained in self-defense the same as Beth, she knew how to distract by words and voice.

Beth saw her chance, but Mr. Calico slapped her hard before she delivered a karate blow. The ceiling light exploded behind her eyes as she fell against the table with a clatter of dishes and silverware, then slid off into the nook's cushioned seat. Mr. Calico held her mother back with the gun while Sarge came under the table, whiff-whiffing in Beth's face and licking her cheek. Pushing the botch hound away angrily she groped up, shaking and very ashamed. A fine policeman's daughter and future police woman! Just a trembling, moist-eyed schoolgirl who was afraid she couldn't take it. Her mother gave her a distressed little smile.

Mr. Calico turned on the radio, and when it warmed up he tuned in the ten o'clock newscast.

". . . and," an announcer was saying, "the second police officer who interrupted the liquor store holdup shot it out with the bandits. He avenged his murdered police partner by killing one of the robbers and seriously wounding the driver of the getaway car before he, himself, was shot down by the third man. That towheaded man is still at large, on foot, but police have thrown a dragnet for blocks around the area and are conducting a house to house search for . . ."

Mr. Calico jerked his towhead around and thrust the gun toward the door from the dark dining room.

"Don't!" Beth shouted. "Billy, stay back!"

But the shuffling sound of the little slippers came right into the kitchen. Her little brother, dark head tousled, blue eyes blinking, almost walked right against the gun.

"A noise waked me," he began.

"Your big sister fell down," said Mr. Calico. "Her thoughts got too heavy for her. Sit down, kid. Looks like your momma has the table set for an evening snack. She'll give you a glass of milk and a cookie after she gets your other sister. You kids can stay up. You got company." He looked at Mrs. Sanders. "Get her, and remember there are two of your kids here with me and the gun." He took the kitchen phone off its cradle. "I'll also be listening in on this extension."

20

Beth nodded helplessly to her mother, and vented her frustrated anger by yanking Sarge closer. Maybe, if her mother or one of the children did make an outcry, he might suddenly realize and prove his worth. Beth doubted it, but it was her only hope. She reached slowly toward Sarge's collar.

"Uh-uh!" said Mr. Calico. "Keep the leash on him."

Beth waited silently until her mother returned with Kathy wrapped in a pink blanket. She shook her head slightly as her mother was about to place Kathy in the nook, between Beth and Mr. Calico, who stood near the door.

"Give your brain a rest, Sis," he laughed, then motioned Mrs. Sanders to place Kathy on the other side of the nook anyway. "Sis may have to answer the doorbell. There's a house to house search on for me. Sis seems to know at least one of the cops. If he comes calling, she'll have to tell him to go away." Beth didn't answer. "You drive a car?" he demanded suddenly. Beth nodded, then quickly shook her head. "I saw you the first time," Mr. Calico said. He squinted at her. "You get too many ideas. So if I do need a hostage to get through the dragnet and roadblocks, we'll take your brother or sister along too. You won't try anything then." He grinned at Beth's mother. "Nothing will happen to them, Momma, if you've brought them up to behave. We'll leave the dog here to protect you and the other kid. What's his name?"

"Sarge," Billy answered, becoming more awake

21

and big-eyed as he possibly began to realize what was going on. His voice strengthened in what might have been a challenge. "He's sort of a police dog too. Anyway, he was given to us by a policeman, and our father was one too. And Beth is going to be one too."

Mr. Calico gave Beth a wry smile. "So that's it! Well, what do you know? I'm in good company. Policeman's wife. Police dog. Police gal-to-be." He laughed. "Maybe I'll be reformed. But don't try it, Sis."

Beth, holding Sarge's leash, rubbed her arm where it hurt from being knocked against the table. Mr. Calico turned to Mrs. Sanders.

"What about the cookies and milk for the kids?" Beth's mother lifted a coffee pot from the stove. Mr. Calico spoke quickly. "Be careful how you handle that hot pot."

"I'm very aware of my children's welfare," Beth's mother replied evenly. She poured coffee for Beth. Their eyes met briefly. If there was any message, Beth didn't get it. She felt sick inside. She gripped Sarge's leash and stared down at him. He was keeping an eager eye on Mrs. Sanders as she moved toward the cookie drawer. As always, his attention was on the wrong things. So it would be up to her if the police came to the front door in their house to house search.

But if they did come, what could she do? Would she be foolishly heroic if she told them there was no fugitive here, but at the same time gave them a

22

signal? Could they do anything to prevent her family from being disastrously involved?

Yet it was her duty to warn them. How many times had her father and Mel pounded that thought to her? Police weren't omni-present. They couldn't be everywhere at once, or know everything. They had to depend on citizens, people with courage, to help them do something about what was right and what was wrong. If Joe Citizen didn't do his part, he couldn't expect to have a good police department or live in a safe community. Crime would go on and on.

But here she was, just sitting helplessly and looking abjectly at her dog. She was afraid she couldn't find a solution the way she would have to if she ever became a police woman. She dreaded the moment when she might have to jeopardize her family's safety because of her duty as a citizen. Or maybe she was dreading having to face up to being an adult. She would be no better than her botch dog who hadn't grown up either.

Sarge suddenly strained at the end of his leash as Mrs. Sanders poured milk and filled a plate with cookies. His claws scratched the floor. His tail beat a tattoo. Eyes bright, ears cocked, he drooled from the corners of his mouth.

Suddenly, he turned his head toward the shaded windows. Beth faintly heard the doorbell ring next-door at the Butlers'. She tensed inwardly. It must be the police who had rung the bell at this hour. They'd be here next. What was she going to do? What could she do?

23

Sarge thumped his rump to sit closer to Billy who had a cookie in his hand. Beth gave her brother an okay nod. He tossed Sarge a bit of cookie. Footsteps sounded in the Butler drive. Leaves rustled underfoot in the backyard. Sarge started to turn his head, but kept one eye on Billy. He gave full attention to Beth's brother when more cookies flipped his way. Mrs. Sanders glanced at Kathy tucked in a corner of the breakfast nook. She held out the plate of cookies to Billy again. Her glance did not meet Beth's but Beth got the impression her mother was listening tensely to the sounds next door and waiting, dreading their coming closer. Mr. Calico held his gun very steady as he stood by the door to the dining room. Beth, listening, tried not to look at the little black hole. Period.

Billy tossed again to Sarge. Gulp. It was gone. And so was Beth inside as she heard footsteps going down the drive. They would come here next! She gave Sarge more leash to let him get closer to Billy.

"Give him some more," she murmured. "He's been a good dog in his own screwball way."

"Easy, Sis," Mr. Calico muttered. "That sounds like your last farewells. Don't do it to your family."

"I'm not that foolish," Beth retorted. "You'd be here with my brother and sister, my mother. Nothing would happen to me. I'd have to live alone with myself."

"That's the idea," Mr. Calico declared. "Just keep all that in mind." He motioned Mrs. Sanders to sit down. "Just to keep you bunched," he said. "Won't have to scatter my shots if——"

Beth clenched her hand around Sarge's leash with the loop of it about her wrist. Perspiring, she got slowly to her feet.

"Maybe," she said in a strained voice, "because Mel spoke to me, they won't even come to the door."

"That should let you off the hook," Mr. Calico began, watching her closely. "Sis," he snapped, "what are you thinking now? I'm not too sure I trust you——"

And then the doorbell rang loudly.

Even though Beth had been expecting and dreading it, the sound shocked her into rigidity. Her mother tensed. Billy froze with his teeth halfway through a cookie. Mr. Calico squinted.

It all happened in a split-second with the sound of the bell. Everyone poised. Everyone except Sarge, the botch dog.

As always, he took off for the front door with wildly scratching claws and boisterous barks. And from where Beth stood, his leash snagged Mr. Calico's legs at the knees. Even with a powerful dog like Sarge and with Beth putting tension on the loop end of the leash, the maneuver couldn't have yanked the feet out from under Mr. Calico. But it did make him glance down and step back, as anyone would.

And Beth, trying to remember everything she'd been taught, grabbed the gun with her free hand and shoved it down and away from her family. Her other hand couldn't make use of judo or karate because of the furious pull of Sarge's leash with the loop about her wrist. But Sarge's powerful pulling helped her shove Mr. Calico off-balance into the dining room. His backward groping foot must have struck Sarge who yelped. Then Mr. Calico went down, thumping his head on the edge of the dining room table. Beth didn't take it for granted he was out. Hanging onto the gun with both hands she cried out to her mother.

"The door, Mother, the door! Let them in!"

Mrs. Sanders, about to join Beth in the struggle, hesitated briefly, then dashed toward the front door. Sarge excitedly tried to follow. He dragged Beth away from Mr. Calico. She frantically tried to get free of the loop. Then Mel and other policemen came charging in with drawn guns and shouting commands to the fugitive. One of them fell over Sarge who whirled about in excited circles with high-pitched barks. His tail slapped Beth across the eyes. The big goof!

The police had less trouble with Mr. Calico than Beth and her mother did in trying to quiet Sarge. Finally he calmed after most of the police and the fugitive had left. Mel and his partner lingered briefly.

"Nice going," he said to Beth, and the way he said it made her glow, and maybe there wouldn't be too much argument later if she still wanted to be a police woman.

"Sarge deserves a lot of the credit," she said, tossing half a cookie. Mel looked dubious. Beth nodded.

"Because I knew what I could count on him to do when the doorbell rang."

"Well—" Mel began slowly.

Mrs. Sanders patted Sarge and gave him another half-cookie.

"Maybe he's not your idea of a watch dog, Mel, but he's wonderful with the children." She glanced at the clock. "It will take all of us . . . will take Beth a while to settle down from this excitement. Why don't you stop by when you go off duty in half an hour? We'll still be up."

"Doing solid geometry," Beth declared disgustedly.

"I'll give you a hand with it," Mel said. Then, eyeing Sarge, he added, "If you think it's safe for me to come in uniform. He is a botch dog, you know. He nipped one of the policemen."

"That's my Beanbrain Sarge," Beth declared. "It probably dawned on him he should nip Mr. Calico, but as usual he botched it."

It Shouldn't Happen to a Dog

LEE PRIESTLEY

SNIFFING the fresh laundered smell of my white jacket as I buttoned myself into it that first morning after my vacation, I was glad to be back. It's only a small town drugstore and I'm only an assistant to the druggist who is my uncle. But before long I'll study Pharmacy and then Unk says the Fortson Pharmacy will be all mine.

Walking up front through the creosote smells of the dog medicines and disinfectants we keep at the back of the store, I knew there wasn't a place in the world I'd rather be. Can you think of a better job for a nosey gal than a small town pill roller?

Sure I'm nosey. Who isn't? I'll admit I like to know what's going on. I like people, all kinds, and I like to know what makes them tick. Some folks put jig-saw puzzles together for fun; I do the same thing with talk and tattle and tell-tale actions.

I'd sauntered up to the rental books and found FEARS AND PHOBIAS tucked in between a whodunit and a love story. You can pick up some interesting stuff in the low-level psychologys done for the low brow. I never miss one. So I stood there skimming. Until I got my elbow jogged.

"Young woman!" Mrs. Muchmore's lips were pressed together and her toe was tapping. "You with your nose in a book and customers waiting!"

So I took my nose out. Betsy, my girl friend who lives next door to Unk and me, was busy at the cash register for the ten o'clock coffee rush, but I heard her giggle. Mrs. Muchmore is one of those busty club women types with her eyeglasses pinned to the northeast corner, but she's a good old girl actually. She handed me a prescription slip rather doubtfully and latched onto her Pekinese. She watched me read the veterinarian's pink slip.

"Doctor Dorn said Ching must have those at once," she told me. "So I thought I'd try here first. But if you don't stock them I can call my veterinarian in the city."

The local vet, Doctor Dorn, had prescribed some ordinary dog vitamins for the pooch. I noticed then that the half-pint dog under his mistress' arm did look kind of peeked-ese!

"We can give you these, Mrs. Muchmore," I said. "What seems to be wrong with the little dog?" I started to pat his head in my best dogside manner but Ching lifted his lip to say he wasn't keen about it. So I put my hand in my pocket.

Mrs. Muchmore sniffed. "Doctor Dorn seemed to think it was faulty diet, but I told him that was simply absurd. Ching eats only specially prepared food under the supervision of myself and my maid."

A poor little rich dog, I thought. "The tablets will be ready in a few minutes," I told Mrs. Muchmore. "Would you care to try today's fountain special while you wait? A double supersundae with crushed strawberries, fresh pineapple and whipped cream?"

"I really shouldn't," she wavered. "There's my diet . . . but I've given up candy and all other sweets. I just can't give up ice cream, too." She wedged herself into a booth. "You may bring me a sundae, young woman."

I grinned when I gave the order to the soda boy, remembering something I'd read in our last batch of rental books. The writer of SO YOU SAY YOU DON'T OVEREAT wrote that fat people (especially women) firmly believe it's gland trouble that makes them take on the extra tonnage. He says fatties believe they don't overeat, because they refuse to remember the snacks they tuck away.

Mrs. Muchmore looked up as Betsy's aunt, Miss Myra Sharpe, came by the booth. "Hello, Myra," she called. "Won't you join me?"

Miss Myra stared at the supersundae I slid in front of Mrs. Muchmore like it might explode. "How can you eat that awful mess, Grace?" She sat down opposite her and spoke to me. "Good morning, Donna. You may bring me iced tea, no sugar and two slices of lemon. Grace, you shouldn't."

"You're probably right," Mrs. Muchmore agreed placidly, spoon in the sundae. "I've given up candy and all other desserts, but not ice cream yet." She

30

eyes Miss Myra's angles. "As long as we're playing a game of Truth, you could do with some padding on your bones, Myra. If you'd eat more, it would do you more good than all those extracts and vitamin pills you take."

"But I don't like milk, or liver, or fruit juices," Miss Myra said. Then she went back to Mrs. Muchmore's poundage. Miss Myra's specialty is solving other people's problems. "There's candy on the desk in your morning room, Grace. In that cranberry glass jar. I saw it," she said accusingly.

"I keep it for Ching." Grace Muchmore looked fondly at the grouchy little dog sitting beside her and Miss Myra looked as if she would love to use a fly swatter on him. "If Ching eats his good wholesome dinner he gets one piece for being a good boy. But I never eat candy myself anymore."

Miss Myra let her eyes underscore her friend's well rounded curves. "Well, you certainly shouldn't. Grace, about that Youth Center committee. Now if I were you—"

I left them there. "If I were you" was in Miss Myra's mouth as often as her teeth. She's one of the efficient people who know how anything on earth should be handled and she dotes on making people uncomfortable and unhappy for their own good. I often wondered how Betsy stood it. Betsy lived with her aunt so Miss Myra could devote plenty of time to bossing Betsy. There were just the two of them since the old Captain, Miss Myra's father, had died of a heart ailment a few months back.

We had the vitamin pills for dogs already packaged, but I put them in one of our boxes in case Mrs. Muchmore should think anything already compounded unworthy for Ching. While I was behind the glass screen around the prescription department, Roger Blessen stopped in with the mail and stood talking to Betsy. When I saw Tom Carson, who's blind, poor guy, come in with his Seeing Eye dog, I went up front. Unk doesn't come to work till afternoon unless I call him that there are prescriptions to fill, so I help with the customers in the mornings.

Miss Myra was probably the cause of the uproar that broke out when I was halfway there. She had come up to the cash register with Mrs. Muchmore and either didn't see or didn't notice Tom's dog, Greta. Miss Myra walked too close to Greta, maybe even stepped on the big shepherd's toes. Anyway Greta yelped and plunged in her harness.

Well! Miss Myra screamed. Roger Blessen, who had been standing with his back to her, jerked around. Then Ching, the grouchy Pekinese, feeling left out of all the fun, leaned out of Mrs. Muchmore's clutch and bit Roger, the innocent bystander! Bit him hard, too, between Roger's belt and his mailbag.

That would have been bad enough but Roger flew to pieces like a bottle dropped in a wash basin. He yelled, he babbled some, his eyes rolled. For a second I thought he'd throttle the dog, or the dowager, or possibly both.

Then Betsy flew around the cash register to Rog-

32

er and I caught onto his other arm. The fire died out of Roger's eyes and he shook his head in bewilderment. Then without a word to Betsy even, he slammed out of the store, almost running, his back stiff and his hands doubled into fists.

Betsy's eyes were bright with tears, poor kid. She and Roger are engaged, although Roger is older than most of our crowd. He had been in a hospital in the city with a terrific thump on the noggin from a car wreck and just before I'd gone on vacation, he'd come home again. Instead of going back to his job of high school math teacher, Roger had started carrying mail. It wasn't the change of job anybody expected and there were more lifted eyebrows than you'd see if you used your knife for peas. There was even more conversation about his nerves and a few whispers about an unstable mental condition. I tried not to let the well-concealed (I hope) torch I carry for Roger influence my opinion.

I finally elbowed out of the uproar at the cash register to ask Tom Carson what I could do for him. He followed me back to the dog remedies counter with one of Doctor Dorn's pink slips. He stood there rubbing his chin kind of thoughtfully while I weighed calcium phosphate for Greta. Doctor Dorn likes to give it to nervous dogs. I admired the beautiful big shepherd as she stood at Tom's knees.

Tom looked down as if he could really see her there. "Greta certainly touched off a riot, didn't she? But what I can't figure, why didn't Ching bite

Miss Myra instead of Roger? She was just as handy and making all the fuss."

That reminded me of the book Mrs. Muchmore had me take my nose out of. I told Tom about it. That the psychologists say fear has a smell. And otherwise peaceful animals will attack without cause the person who gives off the scent of fear. Tom nodded when I finished as if he had heard it all before.

"How did Roger look when he left the store?" he asked me. "Make with the four eyes, Donna."

Everybody in town kids me about being four-eyed. Most of it is because I wear glasses and the rest because I'm snoopy. Anyway I don't miss much. I guess the reason I haven't tried contact lenses is I'm afraid I wouldn't see quite as well.

So I thought about Roger. "Stiff back," I said. "Hands balled into fists . . . a kind of stumbling trot. He kept looking back over his shoulder too."

"A perfect picture of fear," Tom said thoughtfully. "What was he afraid of? I wonder if that head injury—"

On her way to get rid of the tear signs, Betsy heard that. She came back of the screen and tore into Tom. "You can just quit wondering! Roger is going to be all right! The doctors said so. Just because Aunt Myra thinks they should have kept him longer in the hospital—" Betsy glared at Tom as if he could see her anger. "Roger's going to be all right!" Her voice dared us to think different.

Tom's eyebrows went up. "Your Aunt Myra thinks Roger isn't quite . . . quite?"

Betsy nodded miserably, forgetting that Tom couldn't see her. It was hard to remember that he was blind. Tom had been halfway through medical school when he lost his sight and had to come home. He didn't ask for sympathy. With Greta to help him get around he was establishing a good insurance business.

Tom asked another question. "Did the doctors at the hospital in the city suggest outdoor work for Roger? Is that why he took the mail job?"

Betsy's blue eyes grew rounder. "How did you guess? It took me days to get it out of Roger. He won't talk about his injury."

Tom smiled a little. "It seems fairly obvious that handling high school kids would hardly be soothing for a time. Roger would need something quieter and less demanding just now."

"Roger thinks he never will be able to teach again," Betsy said despairingly. "And he won't even talk about when we can get married. I tell him I can keep my job here if a mailman's pay isn't enough, but he won't make any plans. And dogs! Tom, he's simply going to pieces over dogs!"

"You mean Roger is actually afraid of dogs? All dogs?"

"I never noticed about the dogs before Roger was hurt," Betsy said. "He didn't like Prince, Grandfather's old retriever, but neither did I, or Aunt Myra. Prince was so old and cross with everybody except Grandfather that it was hard to like him. And then Roger just isn't the kind of person who goes around patting stray dogs. There are plenty of people like that," Betsy wound up defensively. "Perfectly normal people too!"

"Sure," Tom agreed. "Liking dogs has nothing to do with being normal. And if dogs don't like you, that doesn't make you a villain either. I knew a regular old saint of a minister that any dog felt obliged to take a bite out of. But dogs can certainly make things lively for a postman that doesn't like them. Tempest in a teapot stuff, I suppose. Or a maelstrom in a mailbag!"

"It isn't funny!" Betsy snapped at him. Then the anger died out of her voice. "I suppose it does look funny. Dogs yapping and tearing Roger's pants and chasing him over fences and up trees. . . . He's been bitten three times already. And he's simply going to pieces. You saw how he acted this morning. He's nervous and irritable and he dreads any noise or confusion—"

"Ataxophobia," Tom murmured.

I knew that word meant a fear of noise and uproar. I'd caught it in that rental book, FEARS AND PHOBIAS.

Betsy went on, "He doesn't want to be around people hardly, or go anyplace."

"Touch of claustro'," Tom said.

"I think he's really afraid of everything," Betsy finished.

"Polyphobia. Fear of almost everything," Tom agreed. "If Roger keeps in this dangerous state of tension, he's certain to run on into a condition of polyphobia."

"Does Roger think—" I stopped, wondering how

36

you could ask tactfully if a man thought he was going off his rocker.

Betsy understood what I didn't say. "Oh, Donna I know he does! Aunt Myra keeps after him to go back to the hospital. She has even hinted to me that Roger might get violent. And Roger is afraid he might!"

Then a clattering and banging at the side door interrupted us. The door rattled under a kick and a shrill kid's voice called, "Open the door! Open the door!"

When I got the door open, I saw that it was Jimmy Joe Ferris, our neighbor's eight year old from around the corner on Elm Street. Jimmy Joe's mother is a widow who rents an extra room to Roger. The boy hadn't been able to open the door because he was carrying a tawny puppy in his arms. He came in, stumbling in haste, his face streaked with tears.

He thrust the spaniel at me. "Donna, Donna! Look at poor Spunky!"

I took Spunky out of his arms, knowing as soon as I felt the heavy limpness that the puppy was dead. In my mind I penned up for life the careless drivers who can't spare a second to spare a boy's dog. Then I saw the puppy's tight-locked teeth and the flecks of foam on his lips.

"Give him some medicine, Donna," Jimmy Joe begged. He and I are friends and he thinks I can do anything. "I came with him as fast as I could. He hurts awful, Donna."

"Spunky doesn't hurt any more," I began, hating to tell him the rest of it.

Jimmy Joe's face lighted with hope. "Then he will be all right, Donna?"

One thing I do know about kids. Get it over with. Quick. I bent to put my arms around Jimmy Joe. "Spunky won't hurt any more, honey. Not ever. Spunky is dead."

He burrowed under my chin, sobbing loudly. I blinked pretty fast myself. Then I laid the puppy on the floor and got a clean towel to wrap him in. "Looks like poison," I told Tom softly.

I gave Jimmy Joe my handkerchief for his nose. Then I asked him, "Where did you find Spunky? Was he with you when he got sick?"

Jimmy Joe wiped his nose on his sleeve. "Spunky and me were playing chase-a-stick. Then that ole postman came along the sidewalk. When Spunky ran out that ole postman jumped and kicked at him, the old scaredy cat."

The postman was Roger of course. His route runs up Elm Street and he lives at the Ferrises.

"He said Spunky scared him, running out like that," Jimmy Joe went on. "Then he said he was sorry, the ole—"

"You mustn't call him names," Betsy protested. "Roger's been sick and—"

"That's what Miss Myra said. She came along and she talked to that ole postman and he got madder and madder and then he went away. Miss Myra told me to keep Spunky out of his sight so he couldn't hurt Spunky. She said he was sick and wasn't . . . 'sponsible." Jimmy Joe went on with complete conviction. "But that ole postman did hurt Spunky. I know he did!"

"Roger wouldn't hurt a puppy," I said soothingly. "He brings letters, not poison for little dogs." Too late, I realized what I had let slip.

Jimmy Joe caught at the word of course. "Poison? Was Spunky poisoned, Donna? I did see him chewing something when I was talking to Miss Myra—" He interrupted himself. "Donna, you know old Mrs. Simpson that lives down our street? The one that doesn't like for little boys to climb her apple trees? Well, last week her ole fat dog chased that ole postman up a tree." Jimmy Joe forgot his grief for a moment and laughed. "It sure looked funny. That ole fat dog was barking and snorting and running around and the tree was bending over because it was little and the postman was big. The postman was awful mad when ole Mrs. Simpson made her dog let him down. And that night the ole dog died and Mrs. Simpson told my mother she believed that postman did it." Jimmy Joe's breath caught in a sob. "And I betcha he poisoned my Spunky too!"

I hadn't heard about old Mrs. Simpson's pug but I'd just got back the night before from upstate where I'd been visiting my cousins. Betsy looked at me and nodded miserably.

"It's all over town that Roger poisoned the Simpson dog," she whispered over Jimmy Joe's head. "That wheezy old pug was almost like a child to the old lady."

Jimmy Joe kept sniffing and we all stood there feeling uncomfortable. I couldn't think of a single useful thing any of us could do about two poisoned dogs. Finally Tom told Betsy to keep her chin up, that it would all work out. He patted me on the shoulder and went away with Greta.

Betsy repaired her make-up and went back to the cash register. I washed off Jimmy Joe's tear streaks and took him and the limp body of his pet back home. We gave Spunky a funeral with all the details I could think up. Then I got the boy talking about the new puppies at Doc Dorn's—he runs a small kennel, too—until he was almost cheerful again. Before I left him with his mother, we had arranged to pick out a Spunky the Second the very next day.

I went back to Main then, stopping on the way to buy some cheese and stuff I like for night snacks. I never have to worry about a diet. Unk says I eat so much it makes me poor to carry it. I met Miss Myra in the supermarket, but she was in a rush and went by me with no more than a nod. I thought she probably had a company dinner coming up, for she had fancy groceries and a box of candy in her basket and the butcher was handing her packages of liver and chicken.

I was getting my change when a familiar voice called to me, "Hello, Donna. I didn't know you were back. I've certainly missed you, kid!"

It was Rick Barlow, the lab technician from the hospital here. He's young and smooth and we can talk shop because our jobs almost touch. I carry

40

that torch for Roger, of course, but when he doesn't even notice the extra light, it gives my ego a boost to know that Rick thinks I'm worth a second glance. I'd never get serious over this blood count expert, but I let him admire me.

"Missed me?" I told him. "You mean you missed the meals I let you have on the cuff at our lunch counter."

"Missed me?" I told him. "You mean you missed the meals I let you have on the cuff at our lunch counter."

Rick felt around his ribs. "Do I look as if I'd lost weight?"

"Then who's been trusting you while I was gone? Come on, we have corned beef with mustard sauce and cole slaw on the counter special this noon."

Rick took my sack to carry and came out of the market with me. We made the store before the counter filled up, and started tucking away the food, which is pretty good at the Fortson Pharmacy if I do say so. Unk and I claim we have the only quick lunch in the state that doesn't greasy fry every bite. We have a cook who knows fast food can be good food and we work at variety too. Anyway while we're eating the cole slaw—not made with dressing out of a bottle—I asked Rick what was new.

He lifted an eyebrow along with his fork. "Haven't you heard that your girl friend's boy friend is in the soup? Right up to here?" He ran a finger across his throat.

"I was only gone two weeks. How could Roger get into so much trouble in that amount of time? I heard about the old lady Simpson's pug this morning. You mean there's more?"

"It couldn't have been easy." Rick answered my first question. "And there's plenty more. You know how Doctor Prentiss likes to hunt? And he usually has two or three bird dogs out at his place at the end of Elm Street? It must have been two or three days after you left, Donna." Rick patted my hand. "About the time I really began to miss you."

"About the time Unk cut off your credit, you mean."

"I saw the whole thing myself," Rick said. "It was my day off and I was coming to town. A new dog that Doctor Prentiss had, jumped the fence and ran up to Roger, sniffing at his heels. Roger lost his head and kicked at the dog. Naturally the dog bit him. Doctor Prentiss was at home. He came out and insisted on dressing the bite and tried to smooth things over. But a day or two later all three of his dogs were dead from poison. So who would you think threw the poison in their pen? Doctor can't do anything, for Roger could probably sue him over the dog bite but he's plenty hostile. You can't blame him. Those dogs were valuable."

"They can't actually pin the poisonings on Roger, can they? Are people saying . . ."

Rick cut a piece of corned beef. "People are saying they'd like to know if Betsy didn't slip Roger a few ounces of strychnine from the store here."

"How silly can you get!" I snapped at him.

"You didn't ask me how silly I could get. You asked me what people were saying. And that isn't all either. They're whispering that the poisoning isn't going to end with dogs."

I dropped my fork and glared at him. "That's the most malicious thing I ever heard! Just because a bunch of coincidences point to Roger, it doesn't prove a thing. Except that he's an unlucky, nerved-up—"

"In all the whodunits I read," Rick interrupted, "they call a bunch of coincidences like these circumstantial evidence." He looked at me, his eyes serious. "You'd better work on it, Donna. I sure would hate to see Roger committed as a maniac if he's just playing in hard luck. . . . Even if that would leave you without a secret crush." Rick looked at his watch and whistled at what it showed him. "I have to chop out, kid. Put it on the bill."

All afternoon I kept hearing scraps of conversation that told me Roger really was as deep in the soup as Rick had said. From the swimmy look of Betsy's eyes I knew that people weren't being too careful that the buzz didn't reach her ears too. About four o'clock I got so fed up I picked a book out of the rentals and hid back of the prescription screen. I didn't want to hear any more doubts of Roger's innocence or speculations about his dangerous mental condition.

But I couldn't escape the dogs even there. The book I'd picked at random was TRICKS OF THE

STICKY-FINGERED TRADE. The second chapter was about dognapers who make a business of luring off valuable dogs. Seems a sure-fire lure is shreds of cooked liver in the trouser cuff. It's guaranteed to bring any dog within sniffing distance. I was sick of dogs so I put the book back and went home.

Thinking about Roger and Betsy kept me awake a long time that night. I just couldn't see Roger in the role of dog poisoner. Half dotty with nerves, he certainly was . . . as who wouldn't be in his situation? I suppose an injury can entirely change the personality, but I couldn't see the city doctors letting Roger out of the hospital if such a change had been noticeable. They would have kept him under observation and treatment.

The only way to keep the town from believing Roger was a dangerous maniac was to find the actual poisoner. Flopping around in my bed I tried to tell myself to keep out of it. But I knew nothing could keep me from nosing around.

With all that time lost in midnight meditation, when I fell asleep I overdid it. Opening one eye to look at the clock next morning I was surprised into tumbling right out. It was my day to get down early and already early was late. By the time I fumbled with the buttonless blouses and buckleless flats that always turn up to plague you when you're in a hurry, I heard Roger downstairs with the morning mail.

I heard Miss Myra at the front door too, saying something like "Here's your clean uniform, Roger.

I met the delivery boy at the corner and since I was coming this way anyhow, I brought it along." Roger didn't sound too grateful for Miss Myra's helpfulness as he left to take his uniform in at the Ferris' where he roomed. Miss Myra yoohooed at Mrs. Ferris to ask if she could use the clothes lines in the side yard to air some blankets.

When I came out Roger was standing on the corner passing the time of day with Tom Carson and Greta, his Seeing Eye dog. Miss Myra had hung her blankets on the clothes lines and gone to lean over the fence to put in her ten cents' worth. I was halfway down the walk to join them when Miss Myra screamed. Greta, the big shepherd began to plunge in her harness.

Then the dog staggered into a fall and lay with her teeth grinding and foam flecking her lips. Tom groped for her frantically, down on his knees on the sidewalk.

"What's wrong with Greta? Miss Myra—Roger? Can't you help her? Is that you, Donna? Do something!"

Miss Myra stood rigidly with the back of her hand pressed over her mouth. Roger looked rooted to the ground. That left it up to me. I bent over Tom and the dog but there was nothing I could do.

Tom's hands went quickly and gently over Greta's convulsed body. Then they were still as he felt the shudders under his fingers growing fainter and fainter. His unseeing eyes were blank, but the lines of his face sagged like an old man's. I found

45

out then what people mean when they say their hearts ached. My heart ached for Tom.

"Not only Greta gone," he said in a dead voice as he got to his feet. "My independence too. Without her I'm a helpless blind man tapping with a cane.... Poison again, Donna?"

"Looks like it," I said. "Tom, can't you get another Seeing Eye dog?"

Tom shrugged bitterly. "I don't have the money. They're expensive." He turned on Roger then, his voice biting like acid. "You got even in a big way, didn't you? Killing a beautiful, useful animal because she showed her teeth at you!"

"What do you mean?" Roger laid a hand on Tom's arm.

The blind man shook the hand off furiously. "Don't act innocent! With half the dogs on your mail route dead, you dirty poisoner!"

Tom swung hard—and blindly, of course—at Roger. What was more surprising his fist landed square on Roger's chin and knocked him flat. As he went down, Roger's mailbag spilled letters and small packages all over the sidewalk. He looked so bewildered there sprawled on his back that it was funny. But not laughably funny.

Tom turned away from Roger contemptuously. "Miss Myra? I'll put Greta on your porch until I can send for her."

"Oh, no, I don't want—I mean, wouldn't it be better to carry her around to the grass there in the shade?"

"You go ahead and show me where to lay her."

46

Tom, with an effort, picked up the big limp body of his dog and followed the sound of Miss Myra's footsteps.

Just before they turned the corner of the porch out of sight, we heard her say in an undertone not meant for our ears—only it's a queer thing how people talk loud to the blind as if they believed they were deaf as well—"You mustn't blame Roger too much for poisoning your dog, Tom. He simply isn't responsible. He should be put away where he couldn't do such awful things."

Roger, still sprawled where Tom had flattened him, took Miss Myra's words like another right to the jaw. Then he sprang to his feet, ready to fight somebody. But I was the only one left, standing there in the middle of the spilled morning delivery. I began to pick it up, not saying anything.

When Roger could get the words out he said, "Tom really believes I could poison his dog? And what did Miss Myra mean about me not being responsible?"

I stood tossing a small package addressed to Mrs. Muchmore from one hand to the other wondering what to say to him. Then I pitched the package into the mailbag and told Roger all of it. It seemed to me that it was time Roger knew what he was up against . . . that the whole town believed he was systematically poisoning dogs . . . that he was not responsible for his actions because they were half crazed . . . and that he was too dangerous to be running loose.

I never saw anybody get thunderstruck, but

Roger looked the way I imagine thunderstruck people do. He hadn't heard any of it, not even about the poisoning of old lady Simpson's pug or Doctor Prentiss' bird dogs.

Finally Roger shouldered the mailbag when we got everything picked up and moved off on his route from force of habit. I walked along with him for a way.

"So the whole town thinks I'm poisoning dogs because they nearly drive me crazy on my route?" Roger's laugh was bitter. "I forgot. I'm already crazy. I'm a canicidal maniac!"

It seemed like a good time to ask if he knew why he was so afraid of dogs. I told him what I'd read about the smell of fear. Roger hadn't heard about that but he knew why he was afraid. He pulled back his shirt collar to show me the scars on his throat. The white seams were faint and barely visible so I knew they had been there a long time.

"When I was just a little kid," Roger said soberly, "a big dog nearly tore my throat out. Naturally I was scared within an inch of my life as well as badly hurt. I never got over it. I think now if my mother had given me a cute fluffy puppy to play with I'd have forgotten the whole thing. But she didn't, and I didn't. I'm still afraid of dogs. Fool that I am, I didn't think of dogs as an occupational hazard for a mailman. You must be right about the smell of fear. I can force myself to walk past a dog. Then his nose tells him that my knees are quaking, so he takes a bite out of me."

I had to turn off the route then to go to the store. "Keep your chin up and your knees stiff, pal," I said to Roger. "This thing will go too far and then we'll catch up with the real poisoner."

"A lot of good that will do me when I'm safe in my straitjacket," Roger said.

Betsy wasn't down at the store yet for it had been my day to come in early. But there hadn't been much doing so my lateness hadn't made any real difference. The soda boy had been selling aspirin and toothpaste between making malts and serving coffee. I made up the orders that didn't need a real pharmacist, stuff like vitamins and cod-liver oil and Miss Myra's liver extract.

I grinned a little when I was thumbing through the sheaf of slips filed under Miss Myra's name. They'd got out of order and I had to shuffle through them to find that the liver extract was a proprietary already made up and bottled. I noticed quite a few prescriptions Unk had filled for the Captain, Miss Myra's father. There had been one member of the family she didn't boss. Not any. The old man had a mind of his own and a voice like a bull horn to speak it with. When he let out a couple of notches the pictures danced on the walls, the windows rattled and the neighbors bent before the gusts.

The Captain was a trial to Miss Myra's old maid's neatness and correctness. He was always hunting or fishing and then tramping home wet and muddy to interrupt her committee meetings while he steamed by the fire. "Steam" made me think about the Captain's old dog too. I was even on Miss Myra's side there. Did you ever smell an old Chesapeake retriever drying out after a day in the duck blinds?

But the old dog was gallant and pitiful too. He was deaf and nearly blind but he loved the Captain above comfort and followed him everyplace. After the old man died—and even that was characteristic (the Captain died on the Fourth of July, Independence Day) the old retriever wouldn't eat and one day disappeared. When Roger and Betsy found him, he was dead, grizzled old chin on his paws, lying across the Captain's grave out at the cemetery.

All the time I straightened the slips and put up the orders my mind worried at the poisonings puzzle like a hound with a ham bone. Which reminded me that I hadn't had any breakfast myself. We serve breakfasts, good ones with hot biscuits and special home-made strawberry jam, but I couldn't decide what I wanted. Maybe if I took the checks to the bank . . . got a little fresh air. . . . So I left the store with the soda boy again and started down the street.

As I stepped off the curb, Mrs. Muchmore's Cadillac swooped around the corner with the chauffeur driving like his own house was on fire. I leaped back out of the way, slamming against a lamp post . . . and felt my blouse rip on a rough corner of the service plate.

I caught a flash of Grace Muchmore, her face working and streaming tears, holding Ching in her arms like a baby. I watched the car race toward the veterinary hospital and I knew that the Pekinese was the latest victim of the dog poisoner.

After that I didn't feel like going to the bank and anyway I had to go home for another blouse. On Elm Street I saw Roger coming back from delivering his route. He walked like an old man, his head hunched between his shoulders and his steps dragging and hopeless. Although he didn't know it yet he was in a worse spot than before.

I knew he had been to Muchmore's because I remembered the small package addressed to her that I'd put back into his leather bag after Tom had knocked him down and spilled the mail. That was opportunity. Ching had bitten Roger the day before. That was motive. And if that grouchy little dog died, Grace Muchmore's money and influence would finish Roger. That was certain. . . .

You've had one of those super nightmares where you're caught between death and disaster with a weight tied to each leg? Just like a bad dream I could see what was going to happen, but I couldn't get there fast enough to do anything to prevent it.

I saw Jimmy Joe Ferris come out in the yard just as I caught sight of a movement beside Miss Myra's porch. It was Greta, the Seeing Eye dog that was supposed to be dead! Staggering to her feet, lunging and yelping! I began to run, afraid that she might harm the boy. As I ran I figured that Greta must have gotten enough poison to make her very sick but since she's such a big dog the dose hadn't been enough to kill her. Now she looked like a Demon Hound out of the chiller movies, snapping and frothing and running in crazy circles.

Jimmy Joe stood staring, wide-eyed. I heard him say, "Oh, the poor thing! It's sick."

And he ran toward Greta to see if he could help her. Roger must have seen the boy and the dog at the same time. Scared as he was of all dogs, he probably thought Greta had risen from the dead with double hydrophobia at the very least.

"Stay away from her, Jimmy Joe!" he yelled at the boy, running too. "Get on the porch! Run into the house!"

But Jimmy Joe wasn't paying any attention to that old mailman. He kept on running. Then Greta whirled in one of her crazy circles and boy and dog went down together.

It must have looked to Roger as if the dog had attacked the boy. He snatched one of Miss Myra's airing blankets as he tore past the clothes lines. Making a shoestring tackle, he muffled Greta in the woolen folds and pitched Jimmy Joe to one side in the grass.

Don't think the kid was grateful. He bounced right back at Roger, hammering on him with his fists and yelling, "You let that good old dog outa that blanket, you hear me? Don't you kill it like you did my Spunky!" He was kicking too when I came up and peeled him off Roger.

Greta had grown quiet by the time Tom's sister drove up, bringing him to take Greta's body home. Tom's face was beautiful to see when we brought

52

him a quiet, and very sick but definitely alive dog instead of the stiffened body he'd expected to find. Roger helped me put Greta on the floor in the back of the car.

As he straightened up, Roger spoke to Tom. "I wish you could believe, Tom, that I had nothing to do with Greta's poisoning."

Tom poked a hand—not a fist this time—at Roger. "Of course I can believe it. I didn't really think even at first that you could have poisoned Greta. But it's a human habit to lash out in any direction when we're hurt. So can you forget that right to the jaw?"

When their hands met and Roger stood there with his shoulders back and the first grin on his face I'd seen since I came home, I said aloud what I'd been thinking. "Catching Greta like that took plenty of nerve, Roger."

"I was thinking about Jimmy Joe," Roger said. "Even if he does have me typed for the villain. And Greta wasn't really dangerous. She was sick."

"But you didn't know that," I argued. "Not when you tore into the rescue. You were very brave, Roger."

"Sure," Roger said bitterly. "I'm a big brave hero. The least little pup in town can put me up a tree!"

"Were you afraid when you tackled Greta?" Tom asked.

Roger's eyes began to brighten. "Come to think of it," he said in a surprised voice, "I wasn't scared at all!"

53

Tom nodded. "I thought it might be like that. There's a proverb, 'Grasp a nettle and you won't feel its sting.' Fears are like the nettles, Roger. If you can quit running away from them . . . if you turn around and face the fears . . . they fade away. Every time."

I couldn't feel quite so optimistic as Roger looked or Tom sounded. Give him time and his new outlook on his problem and Roger probably could overcome his phobia on dogs. There still remained the problem of the poisonings. But I didn't open my mouth about Grace Muchmore's Pekinese. I knew Tom would find out soon enough because his sister was taking him and Greta to the vet's. The big shepherd was still a mighty sick dog.

I didn't tell Roger either before he flew off to Betsy like a homing pigeon. There didn't seem any use taking that new spring out of his step or nipping back that new self-confidence before it had a chance to get its growth. I kept hoping that Doctor Dorn could pump Ching's stomach in time to save him.

Then I went on into our house and up to my room to change my torn blouse. I had one arm in it when the whole thing clicked together in my mind. I tell you, I could see the very page in that book SO YOU THINK YOU DON'T OVEREAT! from our rental library. And I knew I had to get to Grace Muchmore's, but fast. There was a good chance of someone besides a dog getting poisoned next.

I hit the stairs like a grade school class boiling

out at three thirty. And the second jump I made broke off the loose buckle on the flats I'd put on in a hurry when I got up late. I felt my foot turn . . . tried frantically to recover my balance . . . tripped on the lost shoe . . . and pitched crashing down the stairs. . . .

Next thing I knew I was staring hard at a calendar on a bare white wall. The silly thing kept insisting that it was the eleventh of the month when I knew it was only the ninth and time to send out the last of the bills. That calendar was two days fast.

"Should keep them wound and set better . . . makes it very confusing," I muttered, shaking my head.

The shake set my head to buzzing like a swarm of bees. Raising a hand to keep it from flying to pieces, I found that I was swathed above the ears in a kind of soft cottony dome. Ah, I thought, the bee hive . . . that's where the bees come in.

Then someone took my hand and held it kind of clumsily. I couldn't focus very well but I decided it must be Rick because the hands were so scrubbed and antiseptic smelling. When he spoke his voice was so husky I couldn't be sure it was he. What would make Rick sound worried?

"You sure had me scared, Donna," he said. "I was almost ready to promise never to charge another malt at the drug store! How do you feel? Maybe I'd better bell for the nurse."

Then I heard a swishing and a rattling punctuated with the clack, clack, clack of flat heels. The noises merged into a starchy nurse.

She strongarmed me flat on my back. "Now, now, mustn't fuss with our bandages the minute we get our beautiful brown eyes open! How do we feel?" she asked brightly.

I started to shake my head but thought better of it. The less that humming beehive was disturbed the better. "How should I feel?" I said feebly. "What am I doing here? I don't even know if I've had croup or cholera."

"We must be better if we can be funny." She rattled over to open a blind. "You fell down stairs at home, Donna. It's a miracle you didn't break your poor neck. Doctor x-rayed for fracture, but it was only concussion." Nurse sounded kind of disappointed in me.

Wobbling, I sat up again. "Then that calendar is right? I've been out cold since day before yesterday?" I couldn't believe it.

"Not unconscious all the time. The last twelve hours were good natural sleep." Nurse pushed back on my shoulders. "But we must be quiet. Maybe Doctor will let us sit up for a little while tomorrow."

Everything came back to me with a rush then. I had to get up! I had to see Grace Muchmore. I fought the blanket off my feet. Nurse began bending me flat again. I got my arms around Rick's neck so I could pull up, but he seemed to misunderstand my intentions. The whole thing was very mixed up when there came another tap on the door.

It was Roger and Betsy. They talked to Nurse in hushed whispers but I could catch what they were saying. "How is Donna? Is she awake yet?"

"Oh my yes," Nurse answered. "We're all right now. You needn't worry about us. You can go in for five minutes while I find Doctor. I think we need a sedative. Don't talk too much."

Betsy and Roger tiptoed in, hand in hand, looking hushed and serious.

"Quit acting like undertaker's assistants," I said crossly. "I'm not dead; just half dead. And don't you believe I was smooching with Rick either. I'm trying to get out of bed and everybody keeps trying to keep me in."

Betsy giggled. "I suppose you don't even know that you and Rick are holding hands?"

Then Roger took my other hand. "We've been so worried about you, Donna."

"Sweet of you," I said sighing. Even holding my hand it was "we" with Roger, and he didn't mean old four-eyed Donna. But I had other problems.

"Listen," I said, "I've got to get out of here."

"Relax, Donna," Roger said. "You have to spend some time being grateful you didn't break your neck. And give Rick another kind of break. How can he be the masculine equivalent of a ministering angel if you won't cooperate?"

I didn't pay any attention to Roger. "Betsy, look

in that closet. Do you see my clothes? Then hand them here and everybody look out of the window."

As I swung my legs over the edge of the high hospital bed I heard the swishing and tapping in the hall outside. I lay back down and yanked the sheet up to my chin.

"All of you follow the leader and don't ask questions!" I hissed at the three of them.

Nurse came in smiling archly. "Doctor will be in to see us in a moment. Promise to be a good girl and I'll ask him if we can sit up for ten whole minutes!"

"What a treat," I said. "Right now, could I have a drink of water, please?"

"Of course." She turned to a vacuum carafe that I hadn't noticed.

I shook my head, starting the bees to humming again. "Oh, no, Nurse. I never drink cold water. Just step into the bathroom there and let the tap run until the water is quite warm."

"Well, for goodness sakes!" Nurse said. But she took the glass and went into the bathroom.

When I heard the sound of the water running I whispered to Rick, "Slam the bathroom door! Lock it!"

All three of them stared at me as if I had gone dotty but nobody made a move. So I clutched the hospital gown around me the best I could, tottered out of the bed and slammed the door myself. I turned the key in the lock and threw the key in the wastebasket. I had to get away.

"Turn your back, everybody," I said. "Until I get decent."

I put on my skirt over the hospital gown. No one could find my other shoe so I went barefooted. By that time Nurse was making several thousand decibels of noise inside the bathroom. I felt like I might fall flat on my face any minute. Roger and Rick and Betsy began to look balky too, so I couldn't give them any time to think about it.

Lucky for me the room was on the ground floor. "C'mon," I said. "Last one out's a rotten egg!"

We dodged out a side door as an orderly came loping down the hall. Nurse was sounding off like a steam calliope in a parade.

After I sat in Rick's little car for a few minutes my head cleared some and the bees toned down their buzzing. "Take me to Grace Muchmore's, please, Rick," I said. "I've got to see her."

They stared at me with their mouths ajar. "Step on it!" I yelped in vexation. "Or Nurse will have us back in our little bed again!"

Betsy's voice shook a little when she answered me. "Mrs. Muchmore is very sick, Donna . . . so sick they haven't moved her to the hospital even. Doctor Prentiss says she has been poisoned. Poor Aunt Myra is prostrated. She's up there now, hoping she might be able to help in some way."

It hit me right between the four eyes. Grace Muchmore was a good old girl, even if she was a bit on the hoity-toity side. Now if she died because my shoe buckle broke—

"We'd better go up to the house anyway," I decided. "And let's go!"

I expected Nurse and the orderly to come boiling out of the hospital any minute. As we wheeled around a corner I thought of something else. "Did the vet save Ching?"

Roger shook his head. "Ching was dead before Doctor Dorn saw him. Mrs. Muchmore had hired a battery of lawyers and it was all over town that I would be arrested. I don't know why I haven't been, unless she got sick too soon to arrange it." He sighed from his shoestrings. "Lord knows if I'll ever get in the clear. I'm about ready to go back to the hospital and ask the doctors to put me in a straitjacket to keep me out of jail."

I saw Betsy's hand tighten over his. "Don't talk like that, Roger. All we have to do is find the real poisoner."

Roger grinned at me. "Prescription: Find poisoner. Get going, Donna. You can do if it anybody can."

I lifted my buzzing head proudly. Roger relied on me. Betsy was first but Donna was good old reliable second. I'd probably get over Roger in time . . . and Rick did have nice eyes.

At Muchmore's the maid looked at us from a tear blotched face when she answered our ring. Grace Muchmore was a good old girl; when your servants love you that's a mighty good sign. Catching a glimpse in the hall mirror of the white beehive bandage on my head and remembering that I was barefooted, I wasn't surprised that the maid stared. But she showed us into the little parlor Mrs. Muchmore called the morning room.

Miss Myra Sharpe turned quickly away from the desk as we came in. She gaped in astonishment when she saw me.

"Donna! Why, I thought you were still in the hospital!"

"They let me out for an emergency." I gave Betsy and Roger and Rick a look that told them to keep following the leader, even if they were sure I had gone off my rocker.

"But your poor head!" said Miss Myra.

I flipped the beehive with a casual finger. "That's the bouffant look in bandages." Then I got serious. "I'm terribly sorry about Mrs. Muchmore's illness. It must be a terrible shock to you, since the two of you are such good friends. I hate to come barging in at a time like this but I had to see you."

Miss Myra looked surprised. So did everybody. I went on.

"Do you remember those tablets Unk put up for your father last summer? The heart medicine? Doctor Prentiss has a similar case now. When Unk went to fill the prescription—it's a standard medication—he found we're out of them. Of course Unk phoned the city and more will come on the afternoon train. But if you could let Unk have the rest of the tablets from the last prescription he filled for your father it would be a real help. We looked up the prescription and found it was filled for fifty tablets the day before the old gentleman died."

Miss Myra fiddled with the catch of her bag, frowning. "I can't recall that there were any tablets left after Father passed on." She shook her head.

"Surely there were," I insisted. "The dose was only one a day."

"Then I suppose there must have been, but I don't remember. Anyway I threw away all the medicines when I cleaned up Father's room afterward."

I shrugged my shoulders. "Well, if you don't have them, Doc Prentiss' patient will have to get along until the train comes in. But Unk thought it was worth trying to see if you still had the tablets."

I wandered aimlessly around the room as I talked, fingering a pile of magazines, straightening the lid on the empty candy jar on the desk, peering into the waste basket. Miss Myra and the others watched me.

"Why don't you want Betsy to get married?" I asked Miss Myra as I casually opened and closed the drawers of the desk.

She stared at me with her mouth open. I repeated the question.

"You certainly are acting queer, Donna," she said then, her voice tart. "I don't think you should be out of the hospital. I have no objection whatever to Betsy marrying. If that is any of your business!"

"It's my business because I'm fond of Betsy," I said firmly. "I want Betsy to be happy. Why are you trying to break up Betsy and Roger?"

"Your choice of words is as unfortunate as your nosiness," Miss Myra said in a huff. "I'm not trying to 'break up' Betsy and Roger." Then her voice became self-righteous. "But I would be doing less than my duty if I didn't point out to Betsy that she would be making a great mistake to marry a man of such violent temper and unpredictable actions. A man who could easily slip over the borderline into—"

Betsy interrupted her aunt then. To my surprise she didn't sound particularly angry and she didn't seem to have noticed that Miss Myra had predicted a future in the booby hatch for Roger. Betsy sounded more thoughtful than anything else.

"You always have been able to get rid of my boy friends, haven't you, Aunt Myra? You found something wrong with all of them . . . something that you were careful to point out to me. Maybe you didn't have too much trouble because I didn't get serious with any of them before Roger."

Betsy smiled at Roger. For some reason I wanted to look at Rick then.

"I always did what was best for you, Betsy," Miss Myra said positively. "When your mother died and I took you and raised you like my own child; when I worked for you, made sacrifices, gave you everything a girl wants, parties and pretty clothes. . . . Why should I let you throw yourself away? Don't you owe me something for all I've done for you, you ungrateful child?"

"Of course Betsy owes you something," I said. "But she's paid that debt a thousand times in love and companionship. She doesn't owe you her entire life."

"I am grateful, Aunt Myra," Betsy protested. "You know I am. I know you've done everything for me. You've managed—" Betsy's face took on a funny look as if she had just stubbed a toe on a surprising idea. *"Managed!* You've managed me just like you do your committees and clubs! You have to prove that you're always right, that you always know best. You don't really care what's best for me or whether I'm happy. You just want to keep managing my life!" Betsy began to sob.

"You'll thank me for it some day." Miss Myra's voice was shrill and her eyes snapped with anger. "It's for your own good! You'll forget Roger after a while. You wouldn't be safe with him, Betsy. Roger should go back to the hospital where they may be able to do something to cure his mental condition." She let her voice drop to a theatrical whisper. "He might even turn against you, Betsy. A poisoner never stops."

"You'd better stop, Miss Myra," Roger spoke ominously. "I took it when you hinted about my sanity . . . even when you accused me of dog poisoning on a grand scale. But you'd better stop hinting that I'm a potential murderer! You'd be clever about it . . . there'd be nothing to connect you with the trail of whispers but I'll know!"

"There's another trail awinding that I want to know about," I interrupted them. "A trail marked with bits of cooked liver with a deadly stuffing of strychnine heart tablets that left dead dogs all along Roger's route. I want to know about a box of poisoned candy—"

"Roger delivered that!" Miss Myra said triumphantly.

The little room was silent as the four of us stared at her. "How did you know about the poisoned candy?" I asked.

Miss Myra shrank back against the wall, her eyes darting in a panic. I couldn't blame her much. The look on Roger's face would have scared me too.

"I don't know what you're talking about!" she said defiantly. "You're making wild guesses. You can't prove a thing!"

My nose kept twitching. There was definitely a strange faint smell in the room . . . a smell that made the hair on the back of my neck sit up. . . . It was the sharp scent of fear that tainted the air. The man who wrote FEARS AND PHOBIAS was right.

"I think I can prove several things," I said. "I saw you buying liver. Everybody knows you don't eat it; you take liver extract." Then I remembered something I'd read in that book called TRICKS OF THE STICKY-FINGERED TRADE.

I took a newspaper off the table and dropped it on the floor. "Stand on that, Roger. And turn down the cuffs of your trousers. Be sure to shake them out good."

Roger was too confused by my actions and words to protest. When he turned down the cuffs of his uniform trousers some dark reddish-brown crumbs fell out on the paper.

"Crumbs of tobacco," Miss Myra sniffed as she edged toward the door.

"Bits of cooked liver," I corrected, signaling Rick to get between her and escape. "You've been planting bits of cooked liver in Roger's clothes ever since he began to carry the mail. You got the liver in the trousers by tricks like taking Roger's uniforms from the cleaner boy and bringing them in when you came to see Mrs. Ferris. No wonder dogs followed Roger around!"

"If that is liver, which I don't for a single moment believe, it could have gotten there any number of ways," Miss Myra said. "None of which have any connection with me."

I thought up some things that did connect with her. "When the vet does a postmortem on Spunky or any of the other dogs that died, he will find strychnine in the same amounts as in the prescription my Unk made up for your father's heart condition—"

A horrible thought had flashed into my mind. I hoped it wasn't true. Suppose the Captain and his old Chesapeake retriever were exhumed? They didn't always think Miss Myra knew best either. Had she assisted them to their graves? I shuddered and turned away from that.

I went on out loud. "You never eat sweets. I heard you say so yourself. So the candy I saw you buy in the supermarket was in that package addressed to Mrs. Muchmore that Roger delivered. You couldn't have known what was in that package unless you had x-ray eyes. Or had sent it yourself. The only way you could get to Ching was through poisoned candy. I'd guess there was a letter with the box—you probably fished it out of the waste basket before we came—supposedly from a confectioner in the city offering a sample of a new line. Mrs. Muchmore put the candy there—" I pointed to the empty jar.

"Later the poor old girl poisoned herself and Ching with her own hand. That book SO YOU THINK YOU DON'T OVEREAT! said most fat people don't notice or remember the snacks they reach for subconsciously. Grace Muchmore was just kidding herself that she had stopped eating candy. She's going to get well for the same reason Tom Carson's dog Greta recovered. They were both too big for the dose."

"Roger did it!" Miss Myra shrilled. "He had to get Grace out of the way! She was going to have him arrested for poisoning Ching!"

Then I saw the smear of chocolate on Miss Myra's thumb.

"That would be convincing . . . if Roger had rushed up here to remove the evidence. But you did. Give me that bag!"

Myra Sharpe backed away from me. But Rick was between her and the door. There was no mercy on Roger's face. Betsy looked at her aunt in stunned horror, then dropped her face into her hands.

Miss Myra wrenched open the bag and crammed a handful of the poisoned chocolates it contained into her mouth. She gulped awfully . . .

choked and swallowed with a dreadful effort . . . found her voice again.

"If Grace had stayed on her diet!" Miss Myra raved. "Then she wouldn't be sick. She made herself sick by her own self-indulgence. And the town is better off without those nasty, dirty dogs! I did it all for Betsy's good. She would have forgotten Roger after he'd been shut up. She would have thanked me! She would have known I was right!"

I couldn't look at her any longer. Sometimes I don't like what I see with my four eyes. . . . I almost felt sorry for the collapsed, groaning woman on the floor. Maybe Doctor Prentiss could get her pumped out in time to save her life. But what was coming to Miss Myra shouldn't happen to a dog.

I turned away, feeling Rick's hand on my arm. I did like what I saw on his face. But that could come later. . . .

The Sensational Type

"FACE it," said grandma at breakfast. "I've been here for three weeks and Fidele hasn't had a single real date so far."

"Oh, Gram," Fidele objected, "don't . . ."

"Well, you *are* seventeen years old, and you are a good-looking girl," grandma said flatly, "and you know what the trouble is?"

"I . . . ?"

"You are too ladylike," said grandma.

"Mother, for heaven's sake! What a thing to say to the child!" Fidele's mother gasped.

"Lydia," said grandma, "you may sit there looking horrified, but you'll have to admit that's a pretty fair description of what is wrong with Fidele."

"I'm not aware that anything is wrong with Fidele."

"Now, let's not get huffy, Lydia. When a girl has hair the color of butterscotch and good brown eyes and nice legs and is seventeen years old, she ought to be creating a sensation somewhere along the line."

"I'm not the sensational type. How can you create a sensation when you just aren't the sensational type?" Fidele asked in her well-modulated, sweet voice.

"Well, you could do a lot of things," said grandma. "But there just isn't anything so terribly wrong with you, honey. You just aren't young enough." Grandma, at sixty-four, wore a grey tweed skirt and a deep red cardigan over a white blouse. Her white hair curled haphazardly around her tanned face. When she did wear a hat it was never a very dignified hat; she was more likely to wear yellow string gloves than white kid ones. For all her sixty-four years she managed to create an impression of youth more vivid than her ladylike granddaughter! Not that Fidele was mousy or somber or anything at all that you could put your finger on. It was simply that her hair stayed neat in a breeze, her loafers never turned over at the heels, she didn't giggle—her poise was beyond her years, and certainly beyond the years of the boys who knew her. She had been a precise little girl, and although it is doubtful that anyone with hair the color of butterscotch could reach the precise spinster age, well, she was missing a lot of fun right now.

"I think I'll send an escort up here for you when I get home, Fidele," grandma announced that afternoon. "A sort of decoy."

"You mean a boy?"

"Yes. Yes, might as well be a boy. One of them ought to be ready to travel by now," mused grandma. "You think you could use a twelve-week-old puppy?"

"You mean a love-me, love-my-dog policy will take years off my personality?"

"With the puppy I have in mind, I can practically see your personality in rompers."

"Let's not go too far, Grandma; but I could use a pup. At least I could take long walks at night, protected."

"Honey, you lay in a supply of dog food. You have a real good chance of becoming the sensational type overnight when this pup arrives."

"What is it, for heaven's sake?"

"Fidele, you put your trust in an old lady. We'll let the breed be a surprise, and if you aren't dated up for the weekend thirty days from now you can trade him in for a nice cat." Grandma had been a member of her local kennel club for at least fifteen years; she had had a French poodle, a Peke and a wirehair that Fidele could remember —and always two Irish setters. All of her dogs were obedience-trained, by herself, and she had a sizable collection of satin ribbons and trophies from both obedience trials and dog shows. There were no canines whose temperaments grandma couldn't describe to would-be dog owners, and Fidele felt sure that whatever breed her "escort" was going to be, grandma wouldn't go wrong in choosing him.

"Ship him up," Fidele agreed. "Mother will

have a fit, of course. When my cocker spaniel died she said that was the end."

"I'll take care of her. You just have to promise me you'll take this puppy for a daily walk, a good long one, and he's yours. Collar included."

Grandma left. Fidele bought a leash and waited. Four days later the express office called Miss Fidele Manning.

"Lady, you got a teddy bear down here," was what the man said. "You want to pick it up or you want we should bring it out on the truck?"

"I'll come down," she said. "I'd rather carry him home myself."

"Lady, you ain't gonna carry this dog home," the voice informed her. "This here dog weighs a good thirty pounds." Thirty pounds? Grandma must have sent an older dog, Fidele decided. Well, then, it would be easy to slip a leash on him and walk to the car. Probably grandma had sold herself on a house-broken, leash-broken dog, and it was going to be much easier to warm mother up to that idea.

"Mother, when you order the groceries get a couple of cans of dog food," Fidele said, by way of heralding the dog's arrival. "Three cans ought to do for today and tomorrow. Monday we can get some more—he might not like one kind."

"Didn't grandma tell you what to feed him?"

"No, but I think he'll have some instructions in his crate." Fidele slipped into a white shirt and a black corduroy jumper and went out to the car. She drove to the express office, her curiosity at the boiling point. Springer spaniel? Nothing sen-

sational about that! Not a boxer? No, not a boxer.
Teddy bear, the man said. She ran through a mental list of fluffy breeds: Collie? Some sort of wolf-
hound? No, grandma wasn't that theatrical. She
parked a block from the express office—as close
as she could get. Quickly she walked to the office.

"You have a dog here for Fidele Manning?"

"Hey," said the young man at the window, ap-
preciatively, looking at her with a long, careful
look. "Are you the one that dog belongs to?"

"Yes, I am. What do I owe for freight?"

"You don't owe nothing. Prepaid." He called,
"Johnson, bring that big dog out here!" In a
moment the crate was set before Fidele. Her pre-
cocious poise slipped. She fumbled with her
thoughts.

"Oh, my golly—I—it's a . . ."

"That's some Saint Bernard dog, lady," said
Johnson. "How old is it anyway?"

"Twelve weeks. He's almost up to my knees,
isn't he?"

"Sure is." Johnson looked at Fidele and grinned.
"Lucky dog!"

Grandma, you were so right! thought Fidele.
She said aloud, "I'll walk him to my car and skip
the crate. It's not a permanent one." She clipped
her leash to the pup's collar. His coat was a
giant-size lamb's wool powder puff with patches of
orange-gold on white. His white-tipped tail flicked
tentatively.

"Good pup!" Fidele scratched him behind one
ear. "Come on, little dog." She tugged gently on

the leash. Too gently—no give! "Here, boy," she insisted, with a slightly less gentle pull. The pup moved his barrel-shaped body a foot forward. His very sad eyes accused her, "It's all your fault." Fidele stooped and sat on her heels to reassure him that the leash wasn't going to be so bad. With an impetuous bound he threw her off balance and licked her face as she sat on the express office floor.

"Hello!" someone's surprised voice greeted her. Fidele looked up to see Ted Walley staring at her in disbelief. Ted would have sworn Fidele Manning would not be anywhere, at any time, sitting on the floor.

"If it isn't Fidele Manning, sitting on the floor," he remarked brightly. "Your dog?"

"Present from grandma." She pushed the pup from her lap with both hands and rose awkwardly. "He's not leash-broke and I guess I'll have to carry him to the car." She put both arms under the pup's legs and lifted him. She felt the unmistakable snap of a slip strap parting from its slip. The pup squirmed and wriggled his forelegs free, which left him dangling from Fidele's arms by his hind legs. She lowered him to the floor. "He's sort of big," she explained.

"He's wonderful," Ted declared, between laughs. "Let me take him to your car, as soon as I pick up a duplicate statement here for dad."

"I'd appreciate the help." She brushed ineffectually at the fine white fuzz that covered her black jumper.

74

Ted, Fidele and the pup covered the block to Fidele's car in less than twenty minutes. Very slightly less, but less. Part of the twenty minutes was spent by Ted's maneuvering the soft, enormous puppy into a carryable position. Part of the twenty minutes was spent talking to people: a little boy who wanted to touch the teddy bear; an old man who had had a Saint Bernard as a child; a middle-aged lady who thought the dog was the cutest thing, and was he part chow? The rest of the twenty minutes was spent coaxing the pup to walk on his leash, because, as Ted conceded, "You can't carry an amorphous mass as big as a full-grown footstool!"

When finally the girl and the dog were settled in the car, Ted suggested, "If you're not busy tonight, I'd like to come over and wrestle with your mutt."

"I'll be busy," Fidele assured him, glancing ruefully toward said mutt, who had begun teething on the seat cover. "But stop by anyway." To herself she said, "Grandma, it's later than you think!"

Fidele smirked rather pleasantly at her mother, who was hurriedly mixing a quart of cooked oatmeal with the remaining half can of dog food. The pup had gulped two and a half cans of food in five minutes and was sniffing expectantly around the kitchen.

"We can't have our baby hungry," mother said.

"Our baby can't possibly be hungry any more. Look at his sides; they're fat as a blimp's."

"He's the sweetest thing I ever saw. Look at that pretty face."

"Mother, I think you're taken in!"

"Aren't you?"

"Yes, and I'm not the only one. He's quite a dog," Fidele said. "Snagged me a caller already."

"He what?" Her mother's eyebrows wrinkled into a frown.

"He and I have a boy coming to call this evening, due to an unladylike performance of mine."

"Don't take grandma too literally, Fidele."

"Well, it wasn't on purpose, but I did take her literally this morning, and it turns out she may not be kidding."

"You're talking in circles. And your slip shows."

"I am? It does?" Fidele, with un-Fidelelike flippancy, whirled across the kitchen floor. The pup scrambled clumsily after her, slid on the waxed linoleum and skidded into the wall nose first.

Ted Walley helped name the pup. He and Fidele explored the possibilities of "Big" and all its synonyms; probed each other's memories for proper nouns having to do with the Alps (no results); considered any number of screamingly funny ideas that weren't funny the second time they tried them out loud. Late in the evening a postman arrived with a special delivery letter from grandma. The postman eyed Fidele's nameless pup suspiciously.

"Will he bite?"

"That's it!" Ted said decisively. "Willie Bite."

"No. No, of course he won't bite," Fidele replied.

76

Grandma's letter included instructions for feeding: to start with, a pound of horse meat and a pound of dry dog meal—every day! The scrawled p.s., which Fidele did not read to Ted, was, "Thirty-day trial! You, too, can be irresistible!"

Willie Bite was the dog's name, and when you call a Saint Bernard by name he perks his ears and inclines his head to one side and looks at you quizzically. Fidele was stopped on the street by three or four persons each day on her terms-of-the-gift dog-walk. Two out of three of them prefaced their remarks about the pup, "Will he bite?" And each time, Willie Bite returned their steady gazes, cocked alert ears and tilted his head as though to ask, "What for?"

Ted Walley loved that dog. Of course, in order to see the dog, he had to see the girl—and actually, she was quite a girl. Ted was not alone in this discovery. Everyone knows a boy's best friend is his dog—or somebody else's dog. Willie Bite introduced any number of boys to Fidele, boys who had known her all along, but had never really looked at the butterscotch hair or the brown eyes. Oh, success came slowly, as it usually does, but it was success. It wasn't going to be necessary to trade the puppy for a cat in thirty days, not at all. But Willie Bite's success was perhaps too successful.

Ted and Fidele played with Willie Bite at home. Ted and Fidele took him walking. They taught him simple obedience and trimmed his whiskers and—or was it the other way around? Ted and Willie

Bite were the pair and Fidele was on a leash—
was it that way? That's the way it was.

You can't go to a school dance on a leash, not
if you're a dog and not if you're a girl. And Fidele
had come to the point where the dance wasn't
going to be interesting in the least unless Ted Walley
took her. The competition was terrific: it was Willie Bite. Ted couldn't see the girl for the dog. He
looked into the brown eyes and said, "Nice expression!" But those brown eyes were Willie Bite's.

Doesn't he ever notice my nice expression?
thought Fidele.

"The color of butterscotch!" murmured Ted.

"That's me!" Fidele hoped. But it wasn't. It
was Willie Bite, losing his puppy fluff and growing
his grown-up coat; his thirty pounds had become
fifty-five and he was four and a half months old,
and grandma was coming to see him.

"Let's give him a bath," Ted suggested. "We
can do it with the hose outdoors. The weather's
warm enough. When's your grandmother coming?"

"Sunday noon," Fidele told him.

"Let's make the bath Sunday morning."

"Oh, goody! Let's!" Fidele's voice had an unfamiliar, brittle tone.

"What's the matter with you?" Ted asked curi-
ously.

"Nothing. Is something the matter with me?"

"Is Sunday morning okay?"

It was fine. A warm Indian summer morning
and what could be finer for a boy and a girl and a
dog? No—a boy and a dog and a girl.

Fidele wore blue denim shorts and a white shirt and nothing on her feet, and something on her mind. Ted wore jeans and a T-shirt and a great big smile of anticipation for a morning with his favorite date. The date wore his tail between his legs.

"Willie Bite'll be dry by ten o'clock," Ted remarked as he dragged the hose into the side yard, behind the tall hedge. "What time do you meet the train?"

"Twelve-five," Fidele answered. "Here, boy!" She urged the pup toward her. "Turn the water on slow, Ted." She picked up the end of the hose and drizzled a thin stream over Willie Bite. "Come on, boy. You gonna get pretty for grandma?" Ted turned the water to a full steady spray and began to rub soap over Willie Bite's neck.

"Look at that big old face," Ted said lovingly.

"Look at that long old tail," Ted said.

"Look at that clumsy old paw," Ted said. "We'll have to enter him in the puppy match October twenty-first."

"That's the date of the dance."

"Look at that floppy old ear! Who's taking you?"

"The Lama of Tibet. Why?"

"No reason. Look at that wet old boy!"

"I said the Lama of Tibet!" Fidele shouted.

"You did?" Ted turned his head just in time to catch the force of water from the hose square in his face.

"Excuse me!" Fidele yelled. She turned the hose down on his head. "Why don't you take me, you— you—dog-lover?" She aimed the water at his shirt.

"Look at me!" Ted wiped his eyes to look. She sprayed the water in his face again.

"What the devil are you doing?" Ted hollered.

"I'm getting you all wet. No, I'm not. You were all wet before I started!"

"Why, you—" Ted grabbed the hose and took aim. Willie Bite ran a circle around them, barking and trailing suds.

The car door opened and grandma stepped out.

"Thank you again," she said to the Conrads, picking up her overnight case. "They'll be so surprised I drove in early." She walked toward the house. "Hello!" she called. "I'm early!" Then she peered around the hedge. A young man seemed to be kissing Fidele. They were both quite wet; in fact, dripping wet. Fidele's Saint Bernard was chasing his tail in a crazy effort to lick some soap suds off it.

"I thought I was early," grandma muttered. "Hello," she called again. "Looks like I'm right on time!"

Love Me, Love My Dog

◆━━━◆━━━◆━━━◆

ARLENE HALE

EVERYTHING was rosy. I mean perfect. I had everything under control. In fact, I challenge you to find a happier guy in the whole Benton High School. I was sitting there gloating over this glorious fact, taking my time with a soda when Malcom Viking sat down beside me.

"Hi, Pete."

"Greetings," I replied.

Little did I know that my hour of fate was quickly approaching. Little did I know that this bliss of mine was about to go up in smoke.

"What's new?" Malcom asked.

That's Malcom for you. Always so different, so refreshing. He's a little runt of a guy who hides behind huge, dark-rimmed glasses. He's not like anyone else in this world, believe me. His sense of humor may be a bit far out, and his brains are in a class by themselves; but otherwise, Malcom's not such a bad guy.

"Malcom, my boy," I said with a broad, smug grin. "Things couldn't be better and if there were something new, I wouldn't want it. I'm happy, happy, happy! Like the birds in the spring, you know?"

Malcom carefully adjusted his glasses and gave me one of his analyzing looks.

"Touch of fever, no doubt. People act like perfect fools just because it's spring! Strange, isn't it?" Malcom sighed.

"Wouldn't hurt you to get a whiff of spring in your tired blood, buddy boy," I said, poking him playfully in the ribs.

Talking of spring, who should walk in the door just then but the loveliest girl I've ever seen. There was a wisp of a blue scarf around her neck that matched her eyes perfectly, and the wind had blown her blonde hair in the most becoming way. I nearly fell off the drugstore stool.

"Hey, dig that!" I whispered to Malcom.

"Who? Her?"

"Yes. Her. Who is she?"

Malcom gave me a disgusted look.

"She's only been in town since Christmas. Her name's Gloria King. I introduced you to her once, remember? She lives next door to me."

"Introduce me again," I said, giving him another sharp nudge. "Suddenly I have a yen for something new after all!"

I couldn't believe that I had ever said hello to this girl before and then had forgotten her. What was I, blind or something? All I know is I was ready to sell all this blissful happiness of mine for one smile from her.

"Oh, Malcòm! There you are!" Gloria called.

I could only sit there, legs gone rubbery, eyes blinking, and voice completely vanished. Gloria plunked some books down before Malcom.

"Would you be a darling and take my books home for me? I've got this silly meeting, and I don't want to lug them around all evening."

"I'll help carry them home!" I blurted out. "Don't worry about a thing, Gloria."

She sent a blue gaze in my direction. "Oh, hi, Pete. Thanks a lot. Bye—"

Then like a leaf drifting on the spring wind, she was gone. I sighed audibly. Can you imagine? She had actually remembered my name. She made it sound like music in my ears. I grabbed Gloria's books and hastily tucked them under my arm.

"Come on, Malcom. We've got a job to do."

Malcom adjusted his glases again and took a deep, ragged breath.

"You're doomed, Pete. If you're thinking of dating Gloria, you've got competition."

"Explain!" I yelled in his ear.

"I'll show you," Malcom smiled in a fiendish sort of way.

I walked so fast that Malcom was out of breath trying to catch up. Malcom cut through the hedge at his house to Gloria's, taking caution to cut a wide circle to her back door.

"There!" Malcom said with a shaking finger. "There's your competition."

My eyes followed Malcom's finger and then I saw it. I jumped back with a gasp.

"What is it?" I asked with a gulp.

Malcom made quite a thing of polishing his glasses on his sleeve.

"Just a dog."

"Dog!" I echoed.

"Hello, Muff," Malcom called, wiggling a couple of fingers at the creature.

The dog got up on all fours, and I'll take an oath that he looked as big as Davy Crockett's bear! He looked like a three-ton heap of sand covered with a 9x12 rug. His feet were bigger than baseball gloves, and his ears drooped on either side of a giant face that held baggy eyes, a tongue a yard long, and one of the fiercest growls I've ever heard. My blood turned to water, and I must confess I hid my six-foot frame behind Malcom's five feet and three inches.

"Isn't he jolly?" Malcom grinned. "I've been over here a few hundred times, and he still doesn't like me. But he adores Gloria and vice versa. Get it?"

"I'm afraid I do," I said weakly.

"If you ever want to hold Gloria's hand, you'll have to hold Muff's paw first. She has a real thing about that pooch."

By now I felt like I had icicles growing down my chest. But never let it be said that Pete Smith turned tail in the face of true love.

"I'll win him over," I vowed.

Bold as brass and as stupid as they come, I

walked right up to Muff without any formal intro-
duction.

"Hello, old boy!" I ventured.

I reached out my hand to pat the dear fellow on
the head, and that monstrous face opened up into
some kind of a yawning pink canyon that had teeth
for mountains and thunder for a voice.

"Nice boy!" I yelled over my shoulder, fleeing
fast.

Malcom, standing safely out of reach of the dear
fellow's chain, only smiled.

"Well, cheerio and good luck and all that."

"Yeah," I gulped. "Yeah!"

Let it not be said that Pete Smith did a second
stupid thing that evening. Indeed not! Instead I
went straight to the library and checked out all
the books on dog care, dog feeding, dog training,
and so forth. I read until I was bleary eyed, but
not one word could I find on how to make a dog
adore me; that is a canine like Gloria's.

Just the same, let the record show that I phoned
Gloria that very evening and made a date for the
next night. After I had done it I sat there shivering, first with delight that I had been accepted
and second with sheer fright, knowing Muff wasn't
going to like me.

I was still shivering when I walked up to Gloria's
front door the next night for our date. She answered
my ring herself and standing beside her, more than
waist high, was this brute of a dog.

"Hello, Pete. Come in. I'll be ready in a minute,"
Gloria said.

I stood there hopping from one foot to the other, wondering how I could get past the barricade, when Gloria laughed.

"Oh, this is my dog, Muff. Be nice to Pete, Muff."

But Muff wouldn't move. All he did was growl.

"Ha, ha," I said uneasily. "I guess he doesn't like strangers very much."

With a fierce tug at his collar, Gloria got him to move, and I perched on the edge of the chair like a nervous parakeet with a cat in the room.

"Nice boy," I murmured.

But Muff wasn't having any of it. I expected to be swallowed whole any minute. It was with a sigh of relief that I got out of that house with Gloria.

"Poor Muff," she sighed. "I hate going off and leaving him. Being chained up all day—well, I know how he feels. I know I'm slightly ridiculous about him, but I've had him since he was a pup."

Malcom hadn't given any misinformation. I could see the writing on the wall. It was love Gloria, love her dog.

"I'd be glad to walk him for you, Gloria," I said.

Gloria squeezed my hand.

"How sweet of you, Pete."

Right then the very last ounce of good sense flew out the holes in my head. How had I ever got into such a mess? I could just see myself trying to take that monster for a walk.

But I didn't envision half of it! When I arrived on the scene the next evening, my poor heart going pitty-pat, I nearly threw the whole business to the winds. But then Gloria gave me another one of those smiles of hers, and I was ready to fight dragons, hurdle mountains, and even walk that dog.

"So nice of you to do this, Pete," Gloria murmured.

"Glad to. Come along, Muff."

Gloria put his leash into my shaking hand. Muff complied with another growl.

"Now you be a nice dog," Gloria said, wrapping her arms around that monstrous head and rubbing the floppy ears.

Right then I nearly barked for attention, too, but I managed to restrain myself.

I'll never know how we got out the door unless it was that Muff pulled me. He understood that when the leash was buckled to his collar, he was to go walking, and it seems that next to eating Gloria's boy friends alive, this was his dearest passion.

Walk? Did I say walk? He tore out of there like there were firecrackers tied to his tail, and there I was, skidding along on my heels, trying to slow him down, and screaming my lungs out at him.

As we whisked by Malcom's house, I saw Malcom leering at us through the window.

"Now, Muff," I said in a coaxing voice. "Be a good dog, Muff!"

He took that as a signal to run harder. So I had to run to keep up. I was beginning to think Muff would never run out of breath, when all of a sudden, he came to a dead halt. I slid into that mountain of a dog, flipped over him, and landed on the other side, first on my head, then on my back. Muff pinned me down with one of those baseball-mitt paws of his and gave me a vicious eye, his cold nose just a fraction of an inch from mine.

I might have been there yet, yelling for help, if it hadn't been for this other canine Muff had spotted. A few unfriendly growls developed, and Muff took off, leash trailing and me still hanging on to the leash.

To be truthful, I don't know how we got stopped. I was only aware that a crowd had gathered, a policeman was blowing his whistle, and Malcom was peering at me like some kind of inquisitive owl.

"Tut, tut," Malcom said. "What kind of chaos is this you're creating?"

I was afraid I would get booked for disturbing the peace. Gloria arrived.

"Oh, poor Muff," she wailed. "Poor Muff."

Not one kind word for my aching bones, skinned elbows, and wounded ego. But I must say, I have a true friend in Malcom. He soothed everything over with the policeman, the neighbors, the three cats, the one dog, and all the bystanders that had gotten into the act.

"I was so hopeful Muff would like you," Gloria sighed, her lovely forehead making a lovely frown.

"You've got to give me a fighting chance! I know Muff will just be crazy about me, once he gets to know me."

"All right, Pete," Gloria smiled. "I think he will be, too."

I almost missed the implication in her voice I was so worn out from my ordeal with Muff. Believe me, it perked me up quicker than all the vitamin pills in the world. I was determined; I was eager. I would work hard. I would be stalwart. Faint heart never won fair canine—I mean lady!

In the next couple of weeks, I was snapped at, growled at, swatted at with a sharp-nailed paw; I was wrapped around trees and telephone poles by his leash; and I was chased by cats, dogs, policemen, screaming housewives, and butchers with hatchet-like knives. (It seems that Muff loves raw steaks and can smell one out as if he were radar-equipped.)

I was dragged across flower beds, nearly sliced to death in front of a power mower, almost run down by a bus, and was becoming a menace to the neighborhood.

"I do think you're making progress," Gloria said encouragingly.

So who was I to give up? I had to keep trying. The next thing was giving the dear fellow his bath. Can you imagine cramming that much dog into a tin tub and soaking him through with water, then scrubbing him with dog shampoo? Not to mention towel drying him, brushing and combing him? Well, I bathed him all right. Muff was downright indignant about it. Maybe I can't blame him. A guy does like a little privacy with his bath. I hate to admit it, but you guessed it! I ended up in the tub, too!

I also spent my money on beefsteak trying to win the dear mutt over. Two dollars and fifty cents' worth could disappear in two swallows! But he liked it. Oh, he loved it! He sniffed around me looking for more. Planting both paws on my chest, he knocked me flat, right into a rose bush. By the time I got out of that, I was scratched from head to foot.

To be frank, I had just run out of ideas when Malcom whispered his sweet nothings into my ear.

"There's a dark cloud on the horizon," Malcom said.

"Yeah?" I growled. "When hasn't there been? I've endured everything there is to endure, and Muff still doesn't like me!"

"What about Gloria?"

"It's hopeless. If Muff would just act human, I know I'd have a chance. And just smell that air! Ah, spring! In spring a young man's fancy—well, you know."

Malcom proceeded to lower the boom.

"Better act fast," Malcom said. "There's a new guy."

"A new guy!" I sat up as if I'd been stuck with a pin.

"Get this. He's the son of a veterinarian who specializes in dog care."

I was beginning to get the picture, and I didn't like what I saw.

"Like father, like son," Malcom said, squinting at me through his glasses.

"Why he'll chloroform poor old Muff or give

him tranquilizers or something! Gloria will be duped. I'm doomed!" I yelled. "Doomed!"

Malcom clapped his hands and stood up.

"Bravo. Bravo! What a performance."

I hauled him down by the shirt collar and glared at him. It's amazing how another's habits will rub off on you. Even a dog's. I planted my nose right against his.

"Listen, that was no act. This is for real. I tell you, Gloria is the light of my life. I can't let any dog lover steal Muff away. I mean Gloria. No, I mean Muff."

Malcom sighed. "What kind of reinforcements have you got for this emergency?"

"None," I confessed. "Absolutely none. Please leave me, Malcom, old buddy. I've got to think. I must be alone to meditate."

Malcom peered at me over the rims of his glasses. "Touch of the fever, no doubt. Queer what spring does to everyone."

Spring! It was everywhere. I walked around the city, staring at the green grass and the leafing trees. Kids were roller skating, jumping rope, and playing marbles. I saw other guys out riding around in cars with their girls, silly grins on their faces. But woe is me. Here I was! Alone!

The new guy's name was Jack. I suppose by a girl's standards he was considered cute. I personally couldn't stand the sight of him. And Muff adored him, simply adored him. But I was certain Gloria liked me. If only Muff would!

Miserably, I smelled spring all around me and

knew that I was about to lose my dream girl because of that silly old dog!

Then the dawn came. One last idea. If this one failed, I was doomed. All it took was a bus ride and a little cash.

Holding my breath, I went to Gloria's that night. Muff was there to greet me with his customary growl. Gloria's eyes widened at what she saw sticking out of my pocket. Then Muff's sleepy eyes flew open, too. That cold nose of his began sniffing.

Then the miracle happened. Muff's tail began to thump against the floor, and for the first time I saw what Gloria saw in that monster. Why he was sort of cute!

I pulled the little dog (obtained from the city pound) out of my pocket and put her on the floor. She was such a little mite, hardly as big as one of Muff's paws. Muff fell all over himself trying to make her welcome. His protective instinct was working overtime. Then the second miracle happened. Muff showed his gratitude like a true gentleman and licked my hand.

"Oh, you've won him over!" Gloria sighed. "I'm glad, Pete. Really glad. I want my friends to like each other. But usually Muff doesn't like other dogs."

"Boy dogs," I pointed out. "But a girl dog—well, that's different. It's spring you know, and 'in spring a young man's fancy lightly turns to thoughts of love.'"

Gloria blushed.

"Now about this Jack that's been hanging around," I said sternly.

"Jack?" Gloria asked vaguely. "Jack who?"

So this story ends happily. If there's any moral to it, let it be this. Persistence does pay off. Don't give up the ship. In other words, faint heart never won fair canine—I mean lady!

Dog Gone

ANDREW HALL

"RE-lax . . . EASY does it . . . stay loose . . . stay loose." Peeps Elliott was on his front porch, coaching himself in loud tones and the terse, staccato directions were a ringing echo of his famous father's style. "RE-lax . . . EEEasy does it."

Assuming the position necessary for "stepping" over the high hurdle, Peeps burst into a shrill whistle of delight. He pushed his weight up on his left toe, flung his right leg forward and upward, pointed the toe of that foot up and held his leg straight. He swung his body low over his right knee and carried his left arm forward and up until his fingers touched the toe of his right shoe. There it was! Perfect form! Well, maybe not perfect, but good, very good and he'd make it perfect.

"Hi there, Mister!" came an unexpected voice from the walk below.

Peeps jumped. Drue Matthews, who was coming for dinner, must have been watching him for several minutes. Peeps rallied fast.

"My worthy woman," he said, "you are looking at the future high hurdle champion of Stephens High School, of Stephens College and maybe of the YOOnited States."

Drue laughed and he looked at her sharply to reassure himself that she had never known of the struggle he had with the race last year. His friend, Stretch Mason, had broken his leg on a hurdle, and it had taken all of Ike Elliott's coaching ability to help Peeps overcome a sudden and real fear of the event. Peeps had not been proud of that fear; he devoutly hoped no one but his father knew about it and he was grateful it was stamped out now.

"Observe the form, Miss Matthews." He swung into position again. Body low over his right knee . . . oh-oh . . . a little stiff there . . . ouch! That hurt! He held it a moment and knew he would be glad when all the kinks were out of his muscles.

In that briefly held second something hit him smartly in the midriff and sent him sprawling on the porch. He wasn't hurt but he couldn't figure what had happened. Drue hadn't moved. Ike—Ike wouldn't attack a guy in a vulnerable position like that. He rolled over and started to get to his knees. He was struck again from behind and flayed his arms to grab a wiggling, struggling little white object. There was a yipping bark and his hands and face were licked by a welcoming tongue.

"Hey!" Peeps struggled to his feet and brought a squirming, excited little mutt into view. "Easy does it, stranger."

Drue came up now and laughed. "My stars, what

an act! Are you hurt?" But she was still holding back more laughter and Peeps knew that unless he was actually broken in two it was still very funny.

"You may pile my bones in the kindling basket," he said coldly. "Did he follow you in through the gate?"

"No," said Drue. "I was as surprised as you were only I didn't let it knock me flat."

They examined the little dog. He was all white, with bright brown button eyes. He was about two feet long and one foot high. His red tongue flicked in and out eagerly searching for a place to lick. His short tail and the part of his anatomy to which it was fastened threatened to wriggle away from the rest of his body. He seemed about to fly apart with joy.

They heard a soft whistle and saw an elderly man coming up the walk.

Peeps said, "That must be your master," and opened his arms to drop the little dog to the floor. Instantly, and with one flying leap, the quivering little creature jumped straight up again and struggled to get a hold on Peeps' chest.

"Why say, you're quite a jumper! All-American, I bet."

The stranger chuckled. "I'm afraid he jumped you when you weren't looking. Hope he didn't hurt you. He can tell a boy's whistle a mile away."

"Is he your dog, sir?"

"Yes and no. We feed him and take care of him but since our son's been away he won't stay home.

Wants somebody to play with. Being in a strange neighborhood—"

"Oh, you're the new people next door."

The man laughed. "Well, I'm half of them. Our name's Church and this is Bandy. So called because he was abandoned by his former owners. He came to us scared and starved and it took a lot of loving to get him out of cringing and belly crawling, I can tell you."

Peeps patted Bandy gently now and said, "I'm Peeps Elliott, Mr. Church, and this is Drue Matthews. My father is Ike Elliott, coach up at Stephens College. Maybe you've heard of him," he finished with the usual singing note of pride in his voice.

Mr. Church said enthusiastically, "Everybody's heard of The Ike. Did Bandy hurt you?"

"Shucks no, just surprised me. I didn't see him come up the walk."

"He didn't," Mr. Church said and there was a note of pride in his voice too. "He jumped the hedge."

Peeps and Drue stared at him.

"He did what? Why that hedge is over three feet high!"

"I know. He did four feet one time."

"Oleo joe! Say, little Bandy, best you join my track team."

The dog was burrowing under Peeps' arm, one eye warily watching to make sure nobody tried to break this up.

Mr. Church gave a demonstration now. He car-

ried Bandy around the hedge and asked Peeps to
whistle for him. Before the whistle was formed
Peeps caught his breath in amazement. Clearing the
height by several inches, came a white, streamlined
figure, whose perfect grace belied the uncertainty
of his ancestors. His front legs were extended, his
back legs whipped out behind, his ears were back,
his short tail rigidly acting as a rudder control.

"Glory be!" gasped Peeps and Drue together and
Peeps caught the dog on the second bounce.

"Looks as if you'd found yourself a pacer," a
voice said and they turned to find Ike and Emmy
watching the show.

Mr. Church returned, introductions were made
and he said apologetically, "This little fellow has
been so lonely he's been sick and I'm afraid he's
adopted your son. I'll tie him up if he bothers you
or if you have a dog that would be jealous."

Ike explained that their dog had been killed several years ago and they had put off getting another.
Ike's work often took him away on trips with the
college teams. Emmy sometimes went with him and
Peeps was farmed out to friends. It seemed a
bit thick to ask people to take in a dog as well as a
hungry boy and they'd decided to wait a while
longer.

They talked more and the upshot was that Bandy
was to eat and sleep at the Churches and then go
wherever his lonely heart dictated.

"The important thing," Ike said earnestly, "is for
us not to feed him. He's a smart little fellow and
he'll soon learn on which side of the hedge his bread

is buttered. As long as a dog has one definite place where he sleeps and eats, he's a happy dog. Once somebody starts feeding him, he sort of expects a hand-out from anybody and he becomes a tramp."

Emmy looked a little uncertain about all this and Peeps saw her frowning. Evidently Bandy saw it too. As if anxious to prove that he would be an asset to any home he went through his string of tricks, one after the other. He sat up, rolled over, said his prayers and then, as if to show he knew that was all pretty average stuff, he turned a complete and very neat somersault.

Peeps' eyes popped with astonishment and his mother burst out laughing. "Oh you darling, we won't let you be lonely!" The friendliness of her tone told Bandy everything was all right and he nearly jumped out of his clean, white skin.

Emmy told Mr. Church they would call soon and he departed, leaving the part time pet with the Elliotts. And in the house, as they all busied themselves, setting the table and getting dinner, Bandy sat quietly in one corner, his bright button eyes following every move Peeps made, his head turning with metronome regularity. Whenever Peeps spoke to him it was as if there were a vibrator in his insides that was agitating his whole body.

After dinner Peeps and Drue wandered down to the drug store for the usual and found the place crowded. They squeezed into a booth with Betsy Conover, Baby Bunting and Lou Fisher. Peeps was in such fine spirits that even the sight of the last couldn't take away his appetite, which it usually did.

Fish was all right, there's one in every school he kept telling himself. He'd tangled with the guy several times, nothing serious, no blood, but Peeps liked things better when Fish was not around.

Todd Matthews, lead off man in the 220 relay, went by and Peeps called, "Yo Todd, how's your time today?" Todd's fingers tightly grasping his nose was answer enough. Everyone laughed and Lou Fisher said, "Now for the sixty-four dollar gimmick, you aren't going out for the high hurdles, are you, Peeps?"

It wasn't a question, it was a statement and there seemed to be a subtle emphasis in it. Peeps was certain Fish didn't know of his unhappy struggle over that event last year and yet, with annoyance, he realized a hot flush was spreading over his face as he encountered Fish's eye. For an anguished moment Peeps wondered if Fish were going to tell the whole loathsome story, with gestures, the way he always did. Peeps didn't want Drue to know about that affair. It was just one of the things he wasn't proud of, and when you like a person you kind of want to put your best foot forward . . . and not in your mouth either. He was eternally grateful to Ike for his help on the deal and he knew now he was in the clear. Unless something dreadful happened, all that miserable feeling was behind him. He could imagine how awful it'd be to sit here and suspect Fish of hidden jabs if it were still true.

He grinned at Fish. "How about pacing me, chum?"

"Me? Pace the high hurdles? You got rocks in

your head? I'm too valuable a man in other events to risk a splat in the cinders."

Peeps laughed. Nothing like knowing your own value, he thought.

When Peeps and Drue left the drug store, there sat little Bandy, his stubby tail beating a happy tattoo. Instantly he fell in behind Peeps and followed along to the Matthews.

At the front door, Drue said thoughtfully, "Peeps, why did Fish even think you weren't going into the high hurdles?"

Peeps felt as if a blast of cold air had been shot into his blood stream.

"How should I know," he said testily. "That guy beats his gums sixteen hours a day and nobody knows the why of it."

Then he turned abruptly, yelled "Ganight!" and broke into the jogging trot he always used in his lonely treks around town, Bandy right beside him. Twice he indicated he wanted Bandy to go over a hedge and twice the little fellow took it like a bird. What a jumper! What a friend! No needling, no belittling questions. Just a good guy. And he had arrived at the right moment to give Peeps a lift—right over the hurdles. Later Peeps dropped into a sleep filled with dreams of Bandy breaking the pole vault record, while thousands cheered. Only two people were silent, Drue and Lou Fisher.

At breakfast the next morning Peeps looked on a bright spring day and his annoyance at last night's needling soon faded.

"How about a little work-out in hurdles this morning, Ike?"

His father looked grim. "I've got to go to the dentist."

Peeps chortled. His own dental visits were behind him for a time and he was enjoying Ike's misery.

"Bzzt . . . brrt . . . bzzt," he began, giving a chilling facsimile of a drill.

"Oh he won't have to have that," Emmy said airily. "He's going to have it pulled."

"QUIET!" yelled Ike.

"I'll go with you and hold your hand," she soothed.

"You do and I'll bite you."

"With your teeth?" Emmy laughed derisively. "Don't be silly."

Peeps called Fly Baldwin to see if he would help him set up hurdles on the high school track. Fly, always loyal and ready, said he was on his way. Peeps went to the front door and received a barrage of flying feet, tail, eager tongue and happy yips, square in the chest and it took three tries to ground Bandy so they could jog off to school together. Fly already had several hurdles up on the outside lane and Peeps, eager to show off his new friend, motioned to Bandy to go over them. Without further orders, Bandy cleared No. 1 hurdle, rocketed along and took 2 and 3. Fly's eyes bugged out and he breathed, "A jumping fool!" They placed the rest of the hurdles in the lane, Peeps held Bandy at the starting line, yelled "Go!" and the little white dog took off as if he had been shot from a gun, and soared with incredible grace over each barrier.

Suddenly Peeps had an idea. He had Fly skip a lane and then they set up the hurdles in the next two. Bandy, leaping for joy at the wonderful time he was having, started to take the hurdles in 3 and 4. Peeps spoke sharply to him. "No, Bandy. No. Over here." He grabbed him and placed him in the outside lane. Again Bandy tried the other lanes, again Peeps took him back. In only a few minutes the smart little mutt got the idea that Lane 1 was his lane, he belonged there and nowhere else.

They got down at the starting line. Fly held Bandy in front of his lane, Peeps got down on his marks in Lane 3, Fly started them.

"On your marks . . . GO!" He opened his arms and released a jet propelled Bandy.

Peeps told Ike later he felt like one of the dogs at a race track, chasing a mechanical rabbit. Bandy took every hurdle at exactly the same height, he hit the ground at exactly the same distance from the hurdle and took off for the next one at exactly the same spot. It was something to see. Unfortunately for Peeps and his shins he tried to see and run too. Finally he settled down and was able to look up the track, to see the hurdles ahead, "step" over each one in turn and only subconsciously watch his pacer, who was always well ahead of him. The sight of the graceful, white body, going over the barriers so easily, inspired Peeps to relax, to stay loose.

They ran the course a number of times until finally Peeps called a halt. Bandy wasn't tired but Peeps was bushed. An enthusiastic crowd had gathered to watch the amazing, hurdling dog. Peeps put him through his series of tricks and the spectators took the intelligent little dog to their hearts.

"I can't think of a better playmate for the Pride of the Elliotts than a stray mongrel." The words were ugly and sneering and could belong only to Lou Fisher.

"I can't either, Fish," Peeps said in his counting-to-ten voice. "Bandy's my mascot. As long as he's around I'll be okay."

Fish laughed, if the sound he made could be called laughter.

"You'd better get your mind on your work, buddy, if you want to be okay. You weren't clearing those bars by much—I mean to be safe."

Peeps realized that Fish had been near him during the entire workout, just watching. Well, nobody was going to unnerve him that way. He looked Fish in the eye for the full count of ten.

"You wouldn't be trying to scare me, would you, Fish? I know how to go over and I'm going. If I fall," here a quick flash of Stretch, down in the cinders made him repress a shudder, "if I fall, I go boom!"

Ike, who had come up with Emmy, said quietly, "You're not going to fall, Peeps. You're doing all right."

Peeps grinned at him quickly. Ike must not get the idea he could be scared by anybody like Fish. "And how'd the dentist make out?"

Ike groaned. "Took my head off."

Emmy laughed. "But luckily your father has two heads so he's fine."

The crowd laughed in appreciation of its favorite couple and straggled off.

Saturday morning, two weeks later, the township schools were having a track meet to determine which contestants would take part in the County Meet. Friday afternoon, late, Peeps came out of the gym and looked for the loyal Bandy. Since the hurdling work-out with the little dog it had been necessary for Emmy to keep him locked in the house until practice was over. Peeps had apologized to Bandy and explained to him that it was just because he won all the races and it made the fellows mad. Always at five Emmy let him out and he broke all records getting up to the school yard to wait for Peeps.

Tonight he wasn't there. Peeps called and whistled, he wandered around the grounds and called and whistled some more. He met Drue and she went in one direction, he in the other, calling and whistling.

"Emmy must have forgotten to let him out," she offered.

"Sure. I guess that's it." But Peeps was worried.

He walked home with Drue and when she said, "Peeps, don't worry about anything, will you? I know you'll qualify for the County Meet," he was grateful all over again that she had never known the terrible fear he had gone through in connection with the race. He wanted to say something about it, now that it was all behind him, but he couldn't. Besides he felt a definite urge to get home.

When he reached the corner of his street he was running much faster than his usual jog and something like panic was crowding his breath so when he burst into the house he could only gasp, "Where's Bandy?"

Emmy looked up in surprise. "He hasn't been here all afternoon. I thought you'd probably locked him up at school."

Peeps' heart dropped. Even Emmy's "Maybe he's at the Churches, he might be sick," didn't help him. He knew, before Mrs. Church spoke that Bandy was not there. She hadn't seen him since early morning.

Nothing Ike and Emmy could say comforted Peeps. He started out and went up one street and down another, whistling and calling, almost sobbing.

"He's so darned friendly," he told Drue and Todd, who were helping him, "anybody could open a car door and he'd hop in and . . . gosh, you know he was awfully mistreated before he came to us and . . ." His voice was husky.

At eleven Ike stopped the search. He said Peeps could not wear himself out that way. The dog was not in the neighborhood and if he'd been picked up by strangers he'd get away and come back. He was too smart to stay kidnapped. He hadn't been injured or they would have found him. Ike had notified the police. Peeps had to eat something and go to bed.

"You have a race tomorrow, you know."

Peeps had forgotten. He stared at his father blankly, then shook his head. His legs felt like lead, the only thing heavier was his heart. How could he possibly run the high hurdles? He couldn't. But if he didn't somebody might think he was still scared and then Fish's hidden meanings would no longer be hidden. Drue would figure it out, everybody would figure it out. Oh my crow, why did things have to get so fouled up? Dead tired and filled with worry he went up to bed and mercifully dropped into an exhausted and dreamless sleep.

Early the next morning he thumped heavily down the stairs and opened the front door. But there was no white flash bounding into his arms. Bandy was gone and Peeps knew that this was the thing, the dreadful thing that could throw him off his race today. He wasn't scared; shucks, he wasn't even thinking about the hurdles, but who'd believe that? A likely tale indeed!

Ike gave him a pep talk before he left the house that should have made him able to hurdle the college tower. Ike wanted him to run the best race of his life and that was a laugh—or a bawl.

He stood around in shivering misery while the other events of the meet were run off. Zip, his own coach, stopped to speak to him. "Don't look now, fellow, but your face is on the ground. Likely to trip you when you start the hurdles." Peeps smiled feebly and knew Ike had sent Zip to try to snap him out of it.

Suddenly it hit him that Drue wasn't there. He hadn't heard her cheerful "Hi!"; he hadn't seen her anywhere. A fine time for her to walk out. Or maybe she'd been kidnapped too, he thought miserably, and then his race was called.

He got in his lane, messed his foot around in the cinders and tried to get a hold. He looked ahead and tried to imagine what could possibly hoist him over that long line of white markers. There were only four entrants in the event. Sacksville was in Lane 4, Kearney High was in Lane 3, Langford in Lane 2 and Stephens in Lane 1. Peeps got down in position and thought he had a good chance of coming in fifth in this little contest. That is if the others couldn't run up and back before he got to the finish line. He put his tense fingers down on the cinders, straightened his arms and lifted his head to look down the outside lane.

There his troubled eyes saw an amazing sight. There was Bandy in Lane 1, just leaving the finish line, soaring with grace and perfect timing over each hurdle, headed straight for him! Peeps dropped on his knees in wonder, the starter told the boys to relax their positions, the crowd cheered and then Bandy whammed into Peeps' chest.

Peeps knew he had never experienced such a lift of spirits, such a surge of energy, such a rush of joy to his heart as he did when a rough little tongue covered his face and arms in ecstatic greeting. Ike was there almost at once, grinning broadly, to take Bandy in his arms and step to one side with him.

All Peeps was actually conscious of, as he waited for the gun, took off and began "stepping" over each hurdle, was the dozens of cold spots left on his face and arms by an excited little dog. He ran easily, the hurdles were no problem, he didn't even think about the hazard they had once seemed. His time was unspectacular but he managed to come in second and qualified for the County Meet. That's what Stephens High wanted and the crowd roared.

Peeps ran straight into the locker room, showered and changed and hurried back to the field. Drue ran up to him at once.

"Oh Peeps that was grand! Todd says your time'll improve and you can win the County."

"How do you know I was grand? You weren't here."

"Oh sure I was. We got here just in time."

"We?"

"Bandy and I. I couldn't sleep last night, worrying about Bandy. From something that was hinted I got an idea. Sure enough I just went down there and whistled and Bandy came. Oh Peeps he was so cute, he jumped out of a garage window. It was higher than four feet, I'm sure, but he got up on the ledge, wobbled for a moment and then just flew at me." She rubbed her chin. "He landed right here."

"Drue Matthews look at me." There was something terrible in Peeps' voice. "Whose garage was Bandy in?"

Drue looked startled, then decided she had said too much and snapped her mouth shut.

"Answer me, Drue."

"Well I'm not going to, so you might as well save your breath. Somebody was just trying to upset you. After that awful experience you had last year why naturally the loss of your dog would ruin your race. And somebody thought that'd be very funny. But it wouldn't have anything to do with being scared or anything."

"What are you saying, Drue?" Peeps' voice was no longer terrible but was filled with a dazed kind of wonder.

"Why you know, Todd told me all about the miserable time you had last year after Stretch was hurt. He said it happens to hurdlers all the time. He told me to help you all I could—so I tried to find Bandy. Because I knew you couldn't run with Bandy lost and it wouldn't have anything to do with being scared—only everybody might not know that."

Oleo joe! Peeps' heart did a couple of nip-ups. Drue had known all along. He needn't have worried about Drue at all. It actually sounded as if a lot of people knew and understood. Glory, glory! Everybody understood just the way Ike said they would. Everybody except—

"Drue, do you think Bandy could find his way back to Fish's garage?" He smiled at her disarmingly. "He left his toothbrush there and I'd like to get it."

Drue laughed and started to answer, then drew herself up stiffly.

110

"No you don't, wise one. You're not going to trap me. I don't know anything about anything. So there!"

Peeps laughed from the bottom of his toes. It was all right. He could settle that score later. And would. In his own way. Right now he felt wonderful. It was spring. Drue was a nice understanding gal and—a wriggling, white object leaped high to hurl itself on his chest and nestle into his shoulder. AND he had the best friend and the best pacer in the YOO-nited States.

Pinafore for Pam

EVELYN WITTER

PAM lifted one blond pigtail to an off-the-ear position and listened carefully at the swinging door between the kitchen and the dining room. Clara had come to help Mom with the Christmas baking a week before Christmas as usual, and as usual they were giving gift secrets away. Pam hated to be an eavesdropper, but it was terribly important to know whether she was going to get a heifer this year or not.

"I figure a nice electric alarm clock would be the best thing I could get Clem this year," Mom was saying. "He's so slow getting up."

"That's nice," Pam heard Clara say, and the electric mixer started whirring again.

"Ice cream maker for Aunt Nell, jeans and pinafore for Pam," Mom went on with her Christmas list.

Pam bit her lip in bitter disappointment. "Pinafore!" she mumbled to herself. There was just no use trying to reason it out with Mom.

The voices went on in the kitchen. "Pam isn't taking baking for 4-H, huh?"

"No, Clara," Mom's sigh was deep. "She wants to start dairy cattle. Starts in January. She figures she could have a yearling to show at the fair in September. Crazy for cattle, and dogs that girl is, and here I was hoping she'd get through that tomboy stage and start thinking about home economics and how to be a girl!"

Without Mom's backing she was practically sunk. Why couldn't Mom understand that a well-fed heifer was much prettier than a plump loaf of bread. More fun and really something as far as the kids were concerned. Jane Parish would never have been elected class secretary if she hadn't won a ribbon at the Dairy Cattle Congress!

The aroma of butter cookies came floating from the kitchen in spite of the closed door. A soft snow was falling like fairy feathers across the bay window and everything in the house hummed of Christmas cheer—everything but Pam. Pam looked at the scenic wallpaper on the dining room wall. Dad said it gave him indigestion, because he was always riding to hunt with the men and horses.

Her eyes narrowed to that scene now and almost changed from brown to sparkling black as they focused on the high fence over which the horses were jumping—fences that looked like the partitions of Mr. Lockhart's calf pens.

Sure, why hadn't she thought of that before! She could get her own heifer! She whirled to the closet, zipped up her jacket, and was just tucking her jeans into her boots when Mom pushed through the swinging door.

"Pam, where are you going! It's almost chore time and you've the chickens to tend." Mom's hair was adorably fuzzy around her face from the heat of the oven, and she smelled deliciously of almonds and vanilla.

"I'm just going to Lockhart's for a minute. You know he always sells his extra cattle around Christmas time, Mom."

Mom wiped her hands on her apron and rolled up her sleeves busily, a gesture Pam had come to recognize as a disapproving, getting down to business one. "Now see here, Pamela Sue," the smooth muscular arm took an upward swing, "I've had about enough of your nonsense. You can't buy a heifer. Why, it takes hundreds, and besides," her voice took on a cuddly tone, "why don't you think about the baking or sewing projects?"

"But, Mom," Pam was adamant, "you said yourself the age of dictators was over and parents shouldn't boss their children, just guide them, and Mom, I want a heifer as bad as—as bad as pigs want corn."

When she saw Mom study her closely for a minute and then lower her eyes, Pam knew she had won her first hurdle at least. "Well, it won't do any harm for you to talk to Mr. Lockhart and look at his heifers, but I don't see for the life of me how you figure—"

Pam dropped a kiss on Mom's smudged lipstick, drew on her skating cap, and walked into the fading day. With Shadow heeling beside her, the crunch of snow singing at her every step, and the clear air filling her with tingling life, she knew that she could not fail. Just through the pasture and under the next hill there was a purebred heifer waiting to be her very own.

She heard a staple "zing" as she climbed over the woven wire fence, which she thought certainly proved what Dad had said about her getting too big to climb over the fences. The Lockhart's red dairy barns festooned in new white were just a few rods away now, and she tossed her braids joyously at the nearness of her prize.

"Mr. Lockhart?" Pam asked at the lighted barn.

"Come in, Pam. Just finishing the bucket feeding." Mr. Lockhart was a big kindly man, always looking in need of a shave. It had occurred to Pam before that if he curried himself down the way he did his cattle, he'd be a fairly decent looking man, even if he was forty or fifty.

"Gee, you've got swell looking calves."

"Yep, I hate to see 'em go. But with good help as scarce as it is—"

"I'd like to buy one," Pam offered. Then as soon as she spoke a chill shook her. Shadow nudged closer as if he too felt doom.

"Well, now," Mr. Lockhart's eyes crinkled up as if he had just heard a great joke. "Which one would you like?"

She dismissed his patronizing tone in the thrill of the moment. Just suppose she could choose one. Which one would it be? She hoisted herself on a box stall railing for a better vantage point and carefully scrutinized the tan Brown Swiss calves.

They were all spring or midsummer calves, all full bodied and straight of back. But there was one —a special one that had a silky fine coat that glistened and shone. Her ears were deep shell pink, and the proportions of her face were perfect.

"That one!"

"You're a good picker, Pam! Just like your dad. That one's out of one of my best milkers, Wardrobe Queen of Hawthorne Knoll."

"That's a strange name," Pam laughed.

"Her hair's so fine and silky. Wears the best coat I've ever seen."

"How much for the heifer, Mr. Lockhart?"

"Well, Pam, I could make her cheap for you," Mr. Lockhart rubbed his chin and the whiskers sounded scratchy. "Let's say two hundred dollars for the heifer and ten dollars for getting the papers and all taken care of."

His words were like a whistle jammed in Pam's ears, and she leaned back to get away from the horrible sound. Her balance beam must have slipped for she felt herself going backward and down fast for an awful moment. She felt herself land in a complete back sprawl on something fairly soft. "Oh-h-h!" Calves bawled and Mr. Lockhart yelled. Her thighs stung and she felt so foolish. Shadow licked her face and his slobber ran down her chin.

"You hurt or something? Here let me help you."

Pam raised from her ungainly repose on the alfalfa and tried to brush her jeans and wipe her chin at the same time.

"No, I'm all right." She tried to make her laughing assured and strong, but it came out thin and stringy. It was hard to be a good sport and businesslike after doing acrobatics with dog slobber and alfalfa leaves dripping all over. Mr. Lockhart didn't help much; he just stood there laughing.

"I'll buy her!" She angrily shouted her deal across the stall. "I can promise you twenty-five cents worth of eggs a day from my own hens."

"Well, now, Pam," Mr. Lockhart grew serious in the face but not in the eyes. "That's a flattering offer, but let's see. At twenty-five cents a day," he started scribbling on the whitewashed wall, "that'd take over two years."

"I could make it shorter with the prize money," Pam pleaded loudly.

Mr. Lockhart cleared his throat and got himself busy letting down more oats in the chute. "I can't sell that way, child. It's sort of the law. Cattle is cash."

"But, Mr. Lockhart," Pam insisted, "isn't there some way we can make a deal for that calf?"

"One way."

Pam's heart started to beat faster. "How?"

"The veterinarian says you got that police dog from him."

"You mean Shadow?"

"Yep. I've always had a liking for that dog. Could use him around the place too. Doc says a hundred dollars wouldn't be too much for him now."

117

"Sell Shadow!" Pam gasped and her head reeled dizzily as she thought of losing him.

" 'Twouldn't be as if you were losing him," Mr. Lockhart read right into her thoughts. "He'd be right here in the barn, and you could come to see him any time you wanted."

"In the barn?" Pam felt that this was an ugly dream, and she would wake up and know that Shadow was hers for always.

"My wife won't have any animals in the house. We'd make him comfortable all right. The barn's warm, especially with all these cattle in here."

"A hundred dollars?" Pam felt she was still in a daze.

"Yep. That's my offer. Leave him here with me as a kind of deposit. I'll keep the heifer for you then. When you pay me for the other hundred from eggs, or prize money, or you could help my wife now and then, the calf will be yours."

"But I'd have to have her in January when the next projects start."

"Well," Mr. Lockhart scratched his whiskers again, "I'd take a couple of your dad's grade cattle for the rest. But the dog's got to be the deposit whichever way we decide."

It was a full clear cold moon that had risen above Lockhart's hill as Pam and Shadow creaked across the pasture for home. The air nipped and bit and aggravated any piece of skin showing. Her thighs ached and the crack of the snow sounded like groans from an instrument that needed tuning. Shadow was cold too and bounded home.

"How'd you make out, Pam?" Mom helped her with her jacket and scrutinized her nervously and with obvious concern.

"No heifer." She wanted to lay her head on Mom's shoulder like she used to do and feel her strong arms cradle her and hear the reassuring phrases in her ear that only Mom could say. But she didn't want Mom to feel worse. She felt bad enough about the 4-H project already.

"Supper's ready, and you don't have to set the table. I tended your chickens, too. Get some nice warm things on, and you'll feel fine when you're warm and full."

After supper Pam did feel better. No mention was made of her visit with Mr. Lockhart. The beef stew that Mom was famous for was better than ever. The cookies were positively melty! Dad was in his finest mood.

Dad! Her last stronghold! She'd approach him farmer to farmer. He sat deep in his chair smiling at the paper. Hogs were up. This was the right psychological moment. She considered sitting in his lap and twirling his forelock. He always liked that. No, she thought, that would disturb that market report. Perhaps it was best to compromise with the paper.

Pam dropped before her father, loosened her hair so that it billowed brightly in the light, and hugged his knees.

"Dad?"

Dad smoothed his hand over her hair like she thought he would and by the time his eyes had

119

traveled to her she was wearing her most benign smile showing the even teeth that he said were like his family's.

"Is two hundred dollars too much to pay for a three-month-old Swiss heifer?"

"Not if she's a good one, it isn't!"

"One of Mr. Lockhart's?"

"Jim Lockhart's got the best herd in the county. Why his father before him was a Swiss breeder." Dad adjusted his paper for punctuation.

"Would you buy one for me?" Pam let it out.

Dad put down his paper. "Now, Pam. I'm for you raising a heifer. It'd be a sound investment. Don't misunderstand me. I think it's good for a girl understanding and appreciating fine livestock, but, honey, why don't you start by raising a grade animal just to start?"

"Oh, Dad! A grade wouldn't stand a chance at the fair. She wouldn't respond to care like a pure-bred. All the others in the club raise good stuff. What chance would I have? And besides Mr. Lockhart's got the most beautiful heifer I've ever seen!"

"Is that so?" Dad smiled.

"Dad?"

"Yes, Pammy girl. What's on your mind, honey?"

"Mr. Lockhart would take Shadow for half the heifer, and he'd take two of your grade cattle for the other half," Pam blurted it all out. She tried to be nonchalant, but her throat got stuck in the middle.

Dad put down his paper with a bang. "Would you give Shadow up?" His eyebrows were raised

120

Pinafore for Pam

high, and his eyes searched hers so hard that she
had to look away.

"I could see him every day. It wouldn't be like
I'd lost him forever."

"If you give up that wonderful dog, I can give
up two calves," Dad said, but his voice was as hard
as last year's corn.

He didn't understand about how important the
heifer was either. She wanted to explain more. She
couldn't bear to have Dad this way with her. But
his paper was up again.

"It's no use, Shadow," she admitted to the dog
who had taken his place beside her bed. "Our lives
are ruined! But please understand about the heifer."
Shadow just gave a sleepy moan which led her to
believe that he didn't really care.

The next morning Pam attached the leash to
Shadow's collar. "It isn't as if we'd never see each
other again," she told him, and when her tear fell
on his nose, he whined.

They made their way over the frosty hill and
back to Lockhart's dairy barn.

"H-here is Shadow," Pam said.

Mr. Lockhart looked up. "Hello there, boy!" he
greeted Shadow with sparkling eyes. He reached
over and stroked Shadow's head lovingly. "He'll
have a good home, never fear."

"Dad says he'll trade," Pam had to hold her face
rigid. If she let it go natural, the tears would all
stream down. She knew she had to hold her feel-
ings in tight or make a terrible scene.

"Fine!" Mr. Lockhart was sure feeling happy. "I'll see him after the sale. Haven't got room right now for the grades. Say, hasn't he got a pretty face?" He couldn't keep his eyes off Shadow.

Pam had to turn on her heels and run. She just had to. She ran all the way home with Shadow's furious barking reaching her, still loud in her ears. The tears streamed down fast—so fast she couldn't see at all. She just found her way home from habit. "Oh-h, Shadow!" she wept out loud. "Shadow, I'll miss you so!"

She was glad Mom was busy in the kitchen when she let herself in the house. She couldn't bear to talk to anyone, not anyone at all!

She ran upstairs, wraps and all, and threw herself across her bed. She had pictures in her mind of Shadow tied in the cold barn. Shadow still barking and pulling on his leash—all confused and sad, wanting to go with the only mistress he'd ever known! She didn't know how long she'd been there crying, for when she woke up it was lunch time.

It was almost impossible to be gay the next day. "Merry Christmas!" all the stacks of mail said. The family put up the tree, and she helped Mom decorate the mantle with bows of evergreens from the woods. There were packages to wrap so gaily, and folk were dropping in with cheerful faces. Mom was bustling to the phone and in the kitchen and getting the special silver and linen ready, and Dad was sneaking about with packages looking like he dictated the hog market. Lockhart's sale bills were all over town announcing fancy heifers for sale the day after Christmas.

But there was no cheer without Shadow. She couldn't bear to go see him. To see him and not have him would be the worst torture she could think of. The house was empty without his faithful company. She never thought about it before, but now she realized what a comfort it was to hear his even breathing at night on the floor beside her bed, to have him close, to talk to him, knowing of the great love he had for her in his faithful heart. Tonight there would be no Shadow.

"Oh, no!" she said aloud without really meaning to.

The food at supper tasted awful. She might as well have had sawdust with her gravy the way the food dried up in her mouth and wouldn't go down. What was the matter with her anyway? She should be happy, knowing she'd have her heifer.

But as the evening gathered she was sadder than she'd ever been in her life. She even forgot to kiss Mom and Dad good night.

But once in bed she even felt worse. All kinds of pictures of Shadow kept coming and coming. Shadow cold. Shadow sad and wondering. Shadow alone with a herd of cows, lying on an unfamiliar bed of straw.

She still couldn't sleep when the big clock in the hall struck one.

"I can't give up my dog!" she said and jumped out of bed, dressed hurriedly, tip-toed down the

123

stairs and out of the house, and made her way to Lockhart's.

She didn't mind the cold at all.

Shadow must have known she was coming, for she could hear him barking long before she got to the barn door.

She switched on the lights and quickly scanned the barn. There in the corner, tied to the last stanchion was Shadow. Straining, jumping, pulling, trying desperately to come at her, no matter how the collar tore into his neck.

"Shadow!" she cried, dropping on her knees and untying the leash.

Shadow sprang at her in his eagerness, his tongue wetting her face and hands. His big paws pushed against her, and his tail wagged and twirled in his ecstasy of joy.

"Shadow," Pam laughed and cried all at once, and her arms encircled his neck and she planted a kiss on his ear. "I'll never, never let you go again. I want my heifer, but Shadow, dear Shadow, I need you."

She scribbled a note on the whitewashed walls. "Mr. Lockhart. I'm afraid the deal is off. Pam."

When they got back home, the lights were all lit.

Mom opened the door. "Pam, where have you been? We've been practically frantic. Your dad's just getting ready to go out and look for you!"

"She's got Shadow back!" Dad stepped forward, and his eyes were soft again. He put his arm around Mom, another around Pam. They exchanged smiling glances.

"Now," said Mom softly, "you and Shadow better get up to bed."

Christmas morning finally came, and Pam prayed that she could go through it the way she should. After all, you couldn't show resentment to people you loved so very much just because they were adults and couldn't understand. She'd open her presents and then walk over to Lockhart's and make one more try—without Shadow in the deal.

"Pam! Merry Christmas!" Mom called from the foot of the stairs and there was a hearty good will in Mom's voice. "And Pam, put on a dress and some decent shoes. After all it is Christmas."

Pam slipped out of her pajamas and drew out from the closet that frilly thing that Mom had made. She knew it made her look all legs and arms, and she hated the way it swished around her knees, but to please Mom—"Here goes," she told Shadow holding her breath as if she were to take a deep dive. "We'll go to Lockhart's later."

Shadow barked understandingly and they descended. There were socks for Dad and the usual atrocious necktie from Aunt Nell. Mom got an electric deep fryer, and then Dad handed Pam a package.

She set a smile, tore at the ribbons as if she were anxious, undid the wrapping, and opened the box. Inside was a frilly pinafore with a piece of paper pinned on the pocket. Her eyes focused on the very official looking print.

125

BROWN SWISS CATTLE
BREEDERS' ASSOCIATION
of the United States of America
56926001
Certificate of Registry
Named: Pinafore for Pam
Owned by: Pamela Sue Kakert
Calved: September 20, 1962
Sire: Lockhart's Brown Buster
Dam: Wardrobe Queen of Hawthorne Knoll

"Why, Mom—Dad—"

Dad chuckled. "Mom insisted on giving you a pinafore, so I told her she could give you the kind she wanted, but I'd give you *my* kind. I'd give you a pinafore from the Wardrobe Queen herself!"

"Oh-h!" Pam just couldn't find words. "Isn't it too wonderful!" was all she could say. "Where is she?"

"In the north box stall, dear," Mom told her, her eyes all shining with happy tears. "You and Shadow go down to see her. We'll open the rest of the presents when you get back."

A Tiger in the House

LORETTA STREHLOW

"JEANIE!"

Margie Wilson, an excited, little dachshund prancing at her heels, burst into the Woodlawn Drugstore and nearly collided with a dark haired man standing at the magazine rack.

"Oh, I'm sorry," Margie grinned but the man didn't smile back. Embarrassed, Margie turned and leaned breathlessly over the soda fountain where her friend, Jean, was working.

"What's the matter, Margie?"

"It's Mr. Phillips, Jeanie. Mrs. Phillips just called to tell me he had an auto accident. Not serious, I guess, but she wants to be at the hospital when he's brought into Riverton and she can't get anyone to take care of Tommy." Tommy was the Phillips' lively six year old with whom Margie and her little dachshund, Tiger, had become fast friends since she'd started sitting with Tommy earlier that summer.

"I told her I'd be glad to help out so she's going to drop Tommy off at my house in just a few minutes."

"Oh, Marge," Jean sighed. "That means you can't go out to the lake with us and a swim would feel so good tonight." She wiped a hand across her damp forehead. "Can't Mrs. Phillips find someone else?"

"They're so new here they hardly know anyone. If it wasn't for Mr. Phillips working for my dad, Mrs. Phillips probably wouldn't have known whom to call. Living out in the old Harris place, they don't have any close neighbors or anything." Tiger dashed madly around Margie's legs, twining his leash securely around her ankles. "Besides," Margie pointed out, "it looks like a real storm coming up. I don't think you'll get to swim either." She bent to untangle the leash and saw the dark man watching her. Straightening up, she headed for the door, avoiding his eyes. "Well, I've got to get home, Jeanie. Have fun if you go."

Margie reached for the door and turned to tug Tiger along. The man at the magazine rack hastily withdrew his foot and Margie knew he'd tried to kick Tiger as they passed. The hair on the tiny dachshund's neck was stiff and Margie felt anger rising. With her cheeks burning, she pushed open the door and ran out. Feeling hot and sticky from the oppressive heat and her own anger, she walked the few blocks to the Wilson home and just opened their door when the phone rang.

"Margie?" It was Mrs. Phillips again, her voice

close to tears. "I don't know what to do. Tommy's still got a slight touch of the measles. I thought it would be all right to bring him to your house but he seems to be running a slight fever and now I don't know . . ." Her voice broke and Margie finished the conversation with a briskness that made her sound older than her seventeen years.

"Don't worry about a thing, Mrs. Phillips. Mom and dad aren't home but I'll leave a note for them and be over as soon as I can."

Mrs. Phillips's shaky voice cleared a little and before she hung up she said, "And please, bring Tiger. Tommy has missed him."

And so Margie had and now she and Tiger were hurrying to close the windows before the rain came. The lightning was coming quicker now, cutting the summer sky into jagged pieces and pulling the thunder behind. She was glad Tommy wasn't afraid of thunderstorms because this one looked as if it might be a bad one.

Tiger ran up the stairs ahead of her to Tommy's room. It faced the back yard where it would catch any stray breeze from the lake but now there seemed to be no wind at all . . . just suffocating heat.

"Hi, Margie," Tommy croaked as she entered his bunkbed domain.

"Hi, yourself. How're you feeling?"

"Kind of warm."

"Isn't everyone," Margie grinned as she sat down on the edge of the bed and lifted Tiger up. The little dog wormed his way swiftly to the top of the sheet and nestled against Tommy, making them both laugh.

"Tiger's not afraid of the measles, is he, Margie?"

"Oh, no. Tiger's not afraid of anything," Margie answered as another roll of thunder split the sky. "Not even thunder like that, are you, boy?"

The rain started then, darkening the sky so that at eight o'clock it seemed like midnight. It fell in such thick curtains that Margie couldn't even see the few homes that were perched on the other side of the open field that separated the Phillips' old house from town. It was as if the three of them were shut off from the rest of the world.

"I think I'll try calling mom and dad again, Tommy." The Wilsons had driven into Riverton for a matinee and planned to come home after an early dinner in the city. "They just might have left the city early to get home before this storm. While I'm downstairs, I'll rustle up some grub. You haven't eaten yet, podner."

"I'm not too hungry."

Tiger leaped off the bed and importantly led the way into the short upstairs hall. Just as they reached the stairs, the phone rang and Margie hurried down to answer it.

"Mom?"

"Margie? No, this is Mrs. Phillips." The line crackled above the storm so that Margie had to strain to catch all the words. "Sedative . . . be hours before Jim wakes up . . . all right but I would like to stay . . . might be all night . . . could you?"

"Of course, I'll stay, Mrs. Phillips. Don't worry about anything. Tommy is fine and if there is anything my folks will be home anytime now and I can call on them."

Still holding the phone, Margie started to dial her own number but Tiger threaded through her legs and whined so that she laughed and replaced the receiver.

"All right, you hambone. I'll feed you and Tommy first. Mom and dad probably aren't home yet anyway."

She knelt to scoop up the little dog and saw that the fur was up around his neck and he seemed to be watching the empty kitchen intently.

"Afraid of the storm, are you?" Margie laughed. "And after I told Tommy how brave you are."

Tiger relaxed in her arms and she carried him into the high-ceilinged old kitchen where she dropped him down while she searched through the refrigerator for something to eat. Remembering that Mrs. Phillips usually kept her canned goods in the recessed shelves that lined the basement steps, Margie recrossed the kitchen into the hallway again and opened the cellar door there.

The stairs were dark, the coolness of the basement refreshing after the heat of the kitchen. Reaching out, she pulled the string that turned on the single bulb at the head of the stairs and picked out a can of soup. Backing out of the door, Margie was startled to see Tiger crouched against the kitchen door. A low growl started deep in his throat and echoed in the empty room. In spite of herself,

131

Margie felt the fine hairs at the nape of her own neck tingle. She shook her head and marched into the kitchen.

"What's wrong with you, Tiger? Storms never bothered you before." The dog whined, his muzzle pushed against the base of the door. "There's nothing out there," Margie said out loud, more to reassure herself than Tiger. "I'll show you."

Gripping the door knob, she swung the door wide, letting in a torrent of rain and blackness. Quickly she slammed it shut again and looked ruefully down at the wet little dog.

"That's what I get for listening to you," she scolded. "A wet dog and a wetter floor."

Mopping up the floor, she heated the soup and carried it up to Tommy. Tiger stayed behind in the kitchen, his long nose still pressed against the door, bright eyes alert to something outside. Tommy was crouched beneath the sheet with the summer blanket pulled to his chin.

"I'm cold, Margie."

It was really dark out now, storm and night combining to black out everything outside the small room. The rain still pounded against the window and the room was excessively warm. Tommy's round face was damp and Margie felt a sudden apprehension.

"Try to eat a little of this warm soup, honey, and you'll feel better." Going into the small bathroom, Margie ran a basin of lukewarm water and sponged Tommy's warm face. After he had spooned a little of the soup and swallowed an aspirin, she tucked

132

the covers around Tommy and went back down-stairs, hoping her parents could be reached.

Tiger left his post by the door and came to stand beside Margie as she phoned. The number rang what seemed an endless time but there was no answer.

Almost nine, a look at the kitchen clock told Margie. Her parents must have been caught in the city by the storm. No telling now when they would get home.

Suddenly, a spear of lightning tore at the sky, lighting up the blackness outside the windows and, for just an instant, throwing the field and houses beyond into relief against the storm. Then the blackness closed in again but not before Margie saw, silhouetted against the window pane, the dark figure of a man. If she made any sound she was not aware of it. The clap of thunder drowned out everything but the thunder of her heart.

How long she stood staring at the window she didn't know but when the next streak of lightning came she saw nothing except the rain and the yard beyond. In a sudden frenzy, Margie ran from the room with Tiger padding warily beside her. As swiftly as she had rushed to close the windows against the storm, now she rushed to turn locks and pull shades against the nameless fear that welled up inside her.

She had locked everything but the room she had fled from. Slowly, forcing herself back down the hall, she entered the kitchen. The dish of scraps she had set out for Tiger still sat on the counter, the soup pan on the stove. Was that someone watching her through the window? She had to know. Boldly, fighting her fear, Margie stepped into the room and across to the window where she had seen the figure. Just then, the storm howled across the open field and sent the wind ripping at the house. The lilacs outside bent to the ground and then whipped violently against the house and scraped and banged against the windows. Margie jumped back as though she'd been slapped and then felt a flood of relief that sent her into hysterical giggles.

"The lilacs," she said to Tiger. "It was only the lilacs brushing against the window." There never had been a man. She let out a rush of breath that made Tiger perk up his ears and look quizzically at her. "Tiger, Tiger," Margie shook her head, "I'm so busy scaring myself that I'm forgetting all about you."

She set the dish of scraps on the floor and turned to the stairs to check on Tommy without noticing that her usually hungry dog was ignoring the supper. He watched the door again and the dark fur around his neck was erect once more.

Tommy's room looked cheerful after the fright Margie had had downstairs in the big, old kitchen.

"Better?" Margie asked, bending over the lower bunk to smile at the little boy.

"I guess so," Tommy answered bravely but Margie could tell by his hot red cheeks that it wasn't so.

"I've got to get a hold of someone," she thought. "A doctor if mom and dad aren't home yet."

She ran down the stairs, nearly falling on the

landing as the lights dimmed and then flicked on again. Outside, the storm seemed to be gaining in intensity, battering against the old house with weird shrieks and whistles that set Margie's teeth on edge. The drawn shades stared at her from the darkened rooms like watching eyes as she hurtled down the last of the steps and fled toward the light of the kitchen and the phone that hung in the hall near it.

"Please. Oh, please, let them be home."

Her fingers shook so that it was hard for her to dial. The busy signal rasped loudly in her ear, shutting out for the moment the noise of the rain. Replacing the receiver, Margie sighed with relief. Tiger came over to rub against her.

"Everything's O.K. now, boy," Margie told him. "At least mom and dad are home. In a few minutes they'll find my note and call or we can get through to them."

Margie shuddered as another gust of wind scrabbled against the windows like sharp fingernails trying to tear into the room. Tiger stiffened, his bright eyes again watching the door leading out to the small porch that fronted the kitchen.

"What's the matter with you?" Margie asked irritably, the sound of her own voice ringing sharply in the high-ceilinged room. "I told you it was just the lilacs, Tiger." The little dog whined and returned to his vigil by the door. Margie felt the same fear she had when she'd thought she'd seen someone at the window. Resolutely, she marched across the floor.

"Once and for all, I'm going to show you there's no one out there, Tiger."

Margie had a hand stretched out to turn the key when the doorknob moved. Slowly, almost imperceptibly it turned to the left and then, just as slowly and silently, back again. Margie stood rooted to the floor, eyes staring in disbelief as the sinister revolving of the knob continued. Sensing Margie's fear, Tiger gave a low growl that broke the circle of fear that had grown in the room. The knob stopped its slow turning, the rain lashed against the door and Margie, her heart pounding in her ears, crept backwards toward the hall and its link to the outside. It was hard to dial when her eyes kept returning to the door but finally she heard the ringing of the phone and then, the deep, comforting voice of her father.

"Hello."

Margie almost wept with joy. Everything would be all right. In a few minutes her father would come and if it was just the wind that had frightened her they could laugh about it but if . . . if someone really was trying to get into the rambling old house she would be safe.

"Daddy! Oh, dad. . . ." Margie's words tumbled over each other, cancelling out the crash of rain and nearly shutting out the tiny click that deadened the line and shut her off from her father and the reassurance of his voice.

"Daddy?"

Her voice echoed hollowly. Margie held the black receiver and stared at it as she had at the turning knob. The line was definitely dead. Had the storm silenced it or was it. . . .

"Margie."

The phone fell from her hand and clattered against the wall. "Tommy! Oh, you frightened me." The little boy stood on the landing in his thin summer pajamas. "What are you doing out of bed?"

"I don't feel so good."

Margie hung the silent phone back on the wall and walked up the steps to hug the little boy. His face was dry and burning to touch, his blue eyes glassy. Her alarm for Tommy made her forget the fears that lurked outside.

"Back to bed for you, young man. Then I'll fix you a nice cold glass of juice."

Picking Tommy up, Margie carried him upstairs. "There you are," Margie smiled, tucking the blanket around Tommy. "Now Tiger will stay with you while I get that juice, won't you, Tiger?"

Lifting the little dachshund onto the bed, Margie walked to the door and closed it behind her. She didn't like to be alone downstairs but neither did she want to leave Tommy alone upstairs. She hurried to the stairs and had just started down when a heavy crash of thunder shook the house and the lights dimmed and then went out altogether. Backed against the wall, Margie felt paralyzed. Her fear had been strong with the lights on . . . with them off she felt almost suffocated by it.

"Margie?"

Feeling her way back up the steps, Margie re-entered Tommy's room.

"It's just the storm, Tommy. The men will find the wires that are down and pretty soon we'll have lights again. I'm going down to find a flashlight or some candles and then I'll get your juice and we'll have a real party up here." She tried to speak with gayety, not wanting her fright to spread to the boy, but Tommy was so feverish he didn't seem to notice. "Tiger will stay with you," Margie reassured Tommy, "and I'll be right back."

She edged her way out of the room and down the dark steps. Since she had pulled all the shades and curtains tight, even the occasional flashes of lightning didn't penetrate the darkness. The Phillips had a gas stove and Margie made her way into the kitchen and toward that. When she found it she switched on the burners, sending dancing shadows into the room. Frantically, she pulled out cupboard drawers, sending showers of towels and silverware raining on the countertop in her search for a light.

Finally, when she had given up hope of finding anything in the kitchen, her fingers touched a loosely wrapped bundle that yielded one long candle and several short stubs. Fixing a temporary holder from a cup, Margie lit one of the stubs. Clutching the other candles, she turned out the stove flames for safety's sake and turned to the refrigerator.

It had stopped running when the lights went out but the candle gave her light to peer within. Finding no juice, Margie straightened up and looked toward the hall where the basement door made a dark rectangle in the wall. Had there been anything she could fix for Tommy on those basement shelves? Yes. She thought she remembered seeing a row of fruit cans and, piled in one corner, some juice.

She stuffed the rest of the candles in the pocket of her skirt and headed determinedly toward the door. The storm seemed to be lessening now, the wind not howling so fiercely at the windows and the thunder rumbling farther away each time.

Margie passed the telephone hanging black and mockingly silent across from the basement door. Surely her parents had discovered her note by now and, not being able to reach her by phone, would be on their way to the Phillips' soon. The thought comforted Margie until she remembered that she had left the note on the kitchen table. If her mother and father had stopped for dinner in the city as they'd planned, they very likely would not go into the kitchen at all. They would think she'd gone to Jeanie's as she'd told them she might. They might not worry about her for an hour or more and then it might be too late . . .

Margie groaned. She was doing it again . . . frightening herself when there might be nothing to be frightened of. All the doors and windows were locked, the storm still raged outside and, more than likely, the figure she thought she'd seen and the turning of the knob were both tricks of the wind. There was no reason for anyone to want to frighten her and she wasn't going to let her imagination do it either.

Taking a deep breath, she held the candle high

139

and pushed open the cellar door. A gust of cool wind lapped at her legs and threatened her candle until she held a cupped hand in front of it. The rows of canned goods marched along the walls, throwing weird shadows that moved with her as she descended the stairs.

She was holding the candle high to read the labels when she first noticed the smell. When she had been in the basement before the air had been heavy with the dampness peculiar to closed basements but now the heaviness was gone, the dampness replaced by the smell of outdoors and rain. Margie's hand reached for a can of orange juice at the same time her eyes followed the feeble light the candle shed at the foot of the stairs and onto the wall beyond. A dark stain started at the foot of the stairs and led back to the wall and up to the single window there . . . to the window that hung open, swinging slightly when the decreasing wind caught it and letting the rain flow over the sill and onto the floor beneath.

Margie never turned her head. Her fingers curled helplessly around the firmness of the can and the other hand held tightly to the cup and its candle. She knew with certainty that she was not alone. Margie wanted to dash the candle to the steps and run out across the wide field to where the friendly houses were sitting but, instead, she forced herself to run a careless finger across the orange juice label as if she were simply considering which can to choose.

Pulling the candle close, Margie forced her face

into a rigid mask so that whoever was watching her from the shadows would think she hadn't noticed the open window. She mustn't let them suspect that she knew they were there . . . waiting . . . watching . . .

Picking up one of the cans, Margie casually turned her back on the darkness at the foot of the stairs and started up the few steps to the safety of the hall. She had nearly reached the top step when the storm outside struck again. The basement window crashed violently, shooting a draft up the narrow stairs that snatched the flame from her candle, leaving her in a pit of blackness. Every muscle froze. She strained to run but was afraid to move. The wind that licked at her legs filled the cellar with sighing that shut out every other sound but the clamor of her heart.

"I must get out. I must," Margie thought desperately. "In another minute whoever is down there behind me will be moving toward the stairs . . . and me . . ."

She took a hesitant step, then another. Behind her, the blackness deepened. She was reaching out a hand for the open doorway when something slid across her face. Dropping the cup with its useless candle, Margie dashed up the last steps and into the hall. Slamming the cellar door, she searched for something to lock it with. Her fingers touched a rusty bolt which she slid home.

"Whoever is down there knows now that I've seen them," she thought weakly. "If only I hadn't let that cord from the light bulb frighten me when it swung against my cheek."

Quickly, without trying to be quiet, Margie slid a heavy chest against the door and then, going swiftly into the kitchen, lit another candle stub. She had to get back to Tommy. Margie paused on her way back past the door. Was there someone behind that rusty lock? Someone listening?

She fled up the stairs and into Tommy's room. Tiger greeted her anxiously at the door, sniffing at her skirt and bristling at what he smelled there. Margie dropped to her knees and buried her face in his fur.

"Oh, Tiger. Tiger, what are we going to do?"

Tommy hadn't moved since she entered his room and, when she held the flame over his bed, Margie could see he was sleeping, breathing heavily and irregularly. The aspirin had finally taken effect but she could see that Tommy was a sick little boy. The rain had stopped beating so hard against the windows and, if she and Tiger had been alone, she would be out and running across the field to safety but with Tommy . . .

"He's too sick to take out in this rain, Tiger. Even if I could carry him . . . no, I've got to think of something else."

Swiftly, Margie let some wax drip on the hard-wood floor and set the candle upright in the middle of the room. She crossed to the door again and pulled Tommy's dresser in front of it. With the dresser between her and the darkness beyond, she stopped to listen. She was glad Tommy was sleeping. At least he wouldn't have to be frightened . . . for awhile anyway. There was no time to waste. Margie knew that her parents were home now, possibly they'd even found her note and tried to call. Somehow she must get a message to them to tell them she needed help. But how?

Tiger moved against her leg, the hair on his neck stiff and wiry, his short, little body pressed reassuringly against her. Margie looked at Tiger and then back to the window. She had an idea but would it work? Quickly, being quiet so she wouldn't wake Tommy, Margie pulled the bedspread and sheet from the top bunk. Tiger stood braced against the dresser as if he knew what was downstairs and was waiting, along with Margie, for the scrape of the chest being pushed across the floor of the hall below.

Margie looped the four corners of the bedspread, tying them together, so that when she held it up, the center of the spread formed a basket. Next, she tied one corner of the sheet around the knots in the spread and fastened it firmly. Going to the window, she pushed it open and leaned out. Yes, attached to the sheet, her basket would nearly reach the ground.

Pulling her head in, Margie searched for something with which to write a note. Probably in the bottom of Tommy's toy chest there would be some broken crayons but there was no time to look. In desperation, she untied the bright scarf she wore around her neck and called to Tiger. He came to her, brown eyes inquisitive, ears alert.

143

"It's up to you now, boy," Margie whispered to him. The little dog whined softly as she wound the scarf around his body and tied it in a loose knot on top. "You've got to take this scarf home . . . home to mom and dad. And if they haven't found my note, you'll have to lead them here."

Margie knew Tiger didn't understand all she was saying but he knew the word home and he knew how to get there from the Phillips'. She and Tiger and Tommy had often walked back and forth between the two homes during the summer. The little boy whimpered in his sleep and Margie thought she heard another sound at the same time . . . perhaps it was only distant thunder, maybe the sound of a rusty lock snapping . . .

"All right, boy. Into the basket."

Margie picked Tiger up and deposited him gently in the center of the spread. He licked her hand and sat very still as if he understood that she was counting on him for something very important.

Margie picked up the spread with its precious cargo and walked to the window. Leaning over the sill, she let the spread down gently on its sheet rope until it swung a few inches from the ground. A warm drizzle fell, shutting out the moon, letting only the lights of the houses across the field glimmer through the mist like lost stars.

"Jump out, Tiger. Out." Her whispered voice sounded hollow after the noise of the storm.

The bedspread quivered and shook and Margie realized that Tiger, with his short legs, would never be able to scramble to the top of the basket. She

144

would have to drop him and hope that he would find his way out of the tangled coverings. Leaning out as far as she dared, she let go of the sheet. It billowed to the ground, falling clear of the spread and Tiger. For a minute the spread wiggled and shivered as if it were alive and then Tiger emerged, the gay scarf still securely about his middle.

"Home, Tiger. Go home," Margie called to him.

The little dog shook himself at the sound of her words, then turned and trotted off in the direction of the road and town. Margie pulled in her wet head and sat down. There was nothing to do now but wait.

It seemed like hours later that Margie heard the first sounds downstairs but she knew from looking at her watch that Tiger had only been gone a little over ten minutes. The rain still fell, not as hard as before, but enough to muffle the sounds of the old house and disguise the movements outside Tommy's room. Margie sat quietly trying to sort out the unfamiliar noises from the ones she knew. How long would the rusty old bolt hold? Once that was broken the chest could easily be moved and then . . .

The stealthy scrape of metal against wood reached her and Margie knew the bolt had snapped. With the fear in her chest almost choking her, she leaned over and blew out the fat candle stump. If someone was in the house intending harm to her or Tommy, they would have a harder time finding the two of them in the darkness.

Minutes passed and then Margie heard the footsteps mounting the stairs. They paused at the landing and then came on. Tommy moaned in his sleep and Margie felt her way to the bed to quiet the little boy. Someone was standing just beyond the door now . . . she could hear the shuffle of feet and a peculiar snuffling in the hall. Sudden anger replaced Margie's fear and she called out.

"Who is it? What do you want?"

Her answer was an excited bark and her father's deep voice.

"Margie? What in the world is going on here?"

"Oh, dad!"

Margie flew to the door and pushed the chest aside. In an instant, she was in her father's arms and Tiger was licking her ankles.

"Oh, dad. I've been so scared." The words tumbled over each other. "There's someone in the house and I was cut off when I got you on the phone and then I didn't know how long it would be before you found the note . . ."

"Wait a minute," her father held out a hand. "What note?"

"Why, the note I left in the kitchen for you and mom. Didn't you find it?"

"No, we didn't. It was Tiger that brought us here. We thought you were with Jeanie and her folks until Tiger came barking at the door. He wouldn't even come in . . . just acted wild when I tried to catch him until finally I got my coat and followed him. Your mother recognized your scarf and called the police. Bud Sawyer met us at the corner and Tiger led us here."

"And a good thing, too," Bud Sawyer's voice cut

through the darkness of the stairway. "A few more minutes and this guy would have gotten away with quite a bundle of things." The young officer shoved a man forward into the beam of Mr. Wilson's flashlight and Margie gasped.

"It's the man from the drugstore." Tiger snarled at her feet and Margie knelt to scoop up the little dog. "He must have heard me telling Jeanie that Mrs. Phillips was bringing Tommy to our house and then, when we came out here instead, it spoiled his plans to rob an empty house."

"I thought I could get in the house during the storm without her even hearing me," the man growled. "Would have, too, if she hadn't had that nosey dog along."

Just then the lights snapped on, clearing the hallway of shadows and waking up Tommy. Margie hurried over to touch his forehead and turned happily back to her father.

"Now everything really is all right. Tommy's fever is down and you're here and . . ."

Tiger wiggled out of her arms and onto the crumpled bed.

"Tiger isn't afraid of measles, is he, Margie?" Tommy asked drowsily as he had earlier in the evening.

"No, sir!" Margie laughed and Tiger joined her emphatically. "Tiger isn't afraid of anything."

The Prize Ticket

◆━━━◆━━━◆━━━◆━━━◆

ANN NAPIER

THE benefit committee of the Christmas dance had decided that each new item on the program should be dovetailed swiftly into the preceding one. So the dance band's last wild note had scarcely wailed away before the chairman, in a few lean movements, was up at the microphone saying, "And now we come to the prize draw. Will the holder of ticket 686 step forward?"

In the hush the chairman artfully produced from somewhere behind his back a small padded traveling basket, such as a puppy uses on journeys. He looked hopefully into the crowd of dancers, standing there in the flag-hung hall, and said again, "Number 686—?" then he flicked open the lid of the basket and a taffy-colored cocker spaniel looked out. "His name is Victory," explained the chairman, "a big name for a very little fellow."

A soft hiss of rapture swept the hall at the sight

of something so small and helpless. There was a movement through the crowd and a slender girl with red-gold hair made her way to the platform. She said, "I have 686," and she held up a square of pasteboard with the figures bold and black upon it.

The chairman was delighted.

From somewhere several camera flash-guns sprayed white, for Belinda Bates, with her flaming hair, milky skin and gentian-blue eyes, was news. Not news in the sense of someone who has done something, but of someone who was something. Her father's daughter. Rich, capricious and petulant.

"Miss Bates," beamed the chairman, moving cunningly into the circle of her influence, where the spotlight was already picking out the red-gold hair, "Miss Bates—" It was going to be a short speech, but with well-rounded phrases; so that when the interruption came, he, too, like Belinda Bates, felt affronted.

The interruption was made by a tall young man who said simply, "Hold everything—" He had dark hair and eyes and a chin that could either be called firm or pugnacious, according to one's immediate inclination. He said, "I have ticket number 686," and he pushed forward a similar square with the same figures plainly marked. Then he stood, legs planted wide, and waited on the fringe of the spotlight.

The chairman clucked beneath his breath, "Some kind of mistake has occurred."

The young man nodded understandingly. "Sure," he said. And then, "The name is Mason."

A flashlight sputtered and the unfortunate situation was preserved for tomorrow's newspaper readers.

The chairman, baffled, remembered Solomon, and wisely decided to forget him again. But Belinda Bates, who had swept through many crises in her eighteen years of merry life, turned her wide smile on the young man. "Oh," she said, with little pretense of sympathy, "how disappointing for you—"

He asked, "Why?"

"Not getting the puppy—" She shook back the red-gold hair.

He said, "I don't follow your line of argument."

"Well," she said, "he'll belong to me—" and she held out her hands for the basket and the dog and laughed the gay laugh that overdrew her banking account.

The young man seemed unaffected by the sound.

This, thought Belinda, is silly. She said, less merrily, "You must realize that he can't be divided up."

"Not physically," he answered.

Belinda was irritated now, and the Mason chin seemed to have advanced unattractively; but the dog was in her arms. The chairman had abdicated, as it were. Indeed, he was already turning to the band, remembering the good plan of the committee to move swiftly from event to event. The band crashed into a lively number. He said, "I am sure we can rely on a friendly solution," and didn't seem to care that his words were smothered by the music. He backed hurriedly away, gesturing to the spotlight to remove itself.

"Well," said Belinda, as she stood, tense, in the returning shadows, "it was nice knowing you," and she turned away from the young man, with a flutter of her skirts, the interlude ended.

But he followed her to the edge of the ballroom, then passed her and, turning, blocked her way. His height was considerably more than hers; his dark eyes were not smiling. He said, "I'll be on your doorstep Tuesday evening at six. The puppy shall spend half the week with me and half with you," and he left her. Over his shoulder, he said, "It may not be friendly, but it's a solution."

Belinda watched him lose himself in the crowd. She tickled the puppy's nose, then she closed down the lid of the basket. She wasn't smiling, either.

She thought, during the next three days, of course he won't come. But, remembering his parting words, she knew he would. And he did.

She had left Victory done up in his traveling basket, and she told the maid to hand him right over. She delayed her dressing, stayed upstairs in a darkened room looking out from behind a curtain to watch him going off. He went. She came slowly down the stairs and felt deserted.

The house seemed even larger than usual: great and echoing. Well, she thought, it was always like this until last Saturday night. It's only since Saturday that it changed at all. She remembered the warm little taffy-colored body snuggling against her; the small clicking noises his paws made on the polished floors, and the innumerable times he climbed up the stairs and remained, in comic majesty, at the top of the flight, powerless to scramble down.

Suddenly she thought, with her blue eyes wide and scared. What if that dreadful young man never returns him, but keeps him forever and ever?

But he didn't.

And it soon fell into a regular routine. Saturday mornings, he came. Tuesday evenings, he went.

And curiosity set in. Who exactly was this young man? There was a goodly column of Masons in the telephone book. She didn't know his first name. There are some things which, if one stays ignorant of them at the beginning, remain a mystery forever. Belinda decided against this type of future. So one Tuesday evening she made up her mind to track him when he returned to what would (presumably) be his home.

She quietly unlatched the door of her house and set out after him through the cold twilight, keeping always a short block behind him. She lurked a little in the shadows, held her coat close up to her chin. And she was, as she imagined, doing a pretty fancy piece of work, when suddenly she knew she had lost him. He was nowhere to be seen. She stopped in her tracks.

And his voice from a doorway called, "Can I help you?"

She thought, only an unpleasant character would startle me like that. And she decided to drop him from her life. She closed her mouth, which had inelegantly come open. She said, "Thank you, but I need no help," and she made to walk on, breaking into an imitation of one who wishes to fulfil an important errand swiftly.

He said, "A simple question would have served your purpose. I would have told you my name was Miles Mason and I live in East Fifty-second Street."

She said, over her shoulder, "I don't care to know."

"Between First and Second Avenues. I have the third floor. I sell stories to 'Glint' and 'Glitter'—and sometimes even to the homier magazines."

She said, "Good evening, Mr. Mason."

He answered, "Good evening, Miss Bates," and she hoped she didn't hear laughter in his voice.

And then one Saturday morning, when the puppy was returned, she found a note tied onto the handle of the basket. She tore it open quickly.

"Dear Miss Bates," she read. "For the first twenty-four hours, while with me, Victory would take no nourishment. I would consider it a favor if you would see that he is not overfed while in your house." It was signed, "Miles Mason."

On Tuesday she replied: "Dear Mr. Mason: It is surprising to me that you do not recognize a state of affairs when it is presented to you. Victory is not overfed. He has never been overfed. If he scorns your food, then it is not his stomach which ails, it is his heart. He is pining for me."

The comeback on Saturday said: "Dear Miss Bates: Your note was as fuzzy an emotional outburst as I have ever seen. Calm down."

She answered him at great length, but the torn

pieces of her letter went into the scrap-basket. At last the four-word note read: "Dear Mr. Mason: Nonsense."

There then followed a period of nothing at all— just the steady succession of Tuesdays and Saturdays and the quick flicking over of the pages of "Glint" and "Glitter," looking for his stories. She thought how well he would write—if he only had a heart. Once she walked accidentally—not too accidentally—down Fifty-second Street, so she now knew exactly where he lived and the color of the curtains. And in odd moments, she taught the puppy how to sit up and beg. He learned quickly. On Tuesday she tied a letter to the basket. It said, "He can beg."

On Saturday, the answer said, "Of course, he can. I taught him."

She replied, "Not you; me."

He answered simply, "I."

And there it rested.

But not too peacefully. She pictured herself as an old, old lady and Miles as an old, old man, white beard waving in the wind, tottering around every Saturday and every Tuesday. Only, of course, that couldn't happen because, by then, Victory would haved died. Died. He couldn't last more than ten years, she supposed. Ten years of this and then— nothing. Just a memory. Less. Actually just half a memory; because he wasn't all hers—as the ticket from the ball kept on reminding her—the ticket with the black numbers, which she could never bring herself to throw away. The Mason half was quite appreciable.

Already, Victory, disguised, had appeared in one of Miles' stories that made a national weekly. The story had been better than anything he'd ever done, even if the heroine did have red hair. She thought, Miles must love her dog. Which was, in fact, true.

For Victory, on his way to becoming a large and amiable dog, interfered considerably with Miles' ordinary routine; and yet Miles never seemed to resent it. When Tuesday evenings came, he would have his eye on the clock keenly; and on Saturday mornings, he would wake up with a vague feeling of depression. And in between, he stood in grave danger of being the young writer who had cornered the red-headed-girl-with-spaniel market.

Although the situation was not improving, it was not until one particular Tuesday that he felt he might do something constructive about it. At the time he was standing in his kitchenette, almost wedged between the sink and the stove, preparing a stew as an appetizing welcome for Victory on his arrival. The idea had come to him with the clear white brilliance of the electric light bulb that flooded the room with harsh light. His jaw set firm and hard. He stirred the mixture; the aroma drifted pleasantly around him. The details of the plan would have to be worked out, but the bare outline was there. This half-and-half life must stop. Even at the price of sacrificing his share of the dog.

If Belinda really loved the puppy, she should have him; and if not, then he would take the dog for keeps.

He would just have to think up a test, for she'd have to prove her love.

He turned the gas off and closed the smell of the stew up in the kitchenette. Then he reached for his hat and let himself out of the door. It was a quarter of six.

A fine rain was falling as Belinda, with Victory on his leash, turned toward her home. Down the narrow street, where the trees were still unleafed, she walked slowly.

Always, as Tuesday drew to evening, she had this leaden feeling of depression, but Saturday mornings were bright again with anticipation. And so the weeks kept up their continual see-saw. She realized that, brooding on the approaching separation, she had slackened her pace. It was already five minutes of six. She'd be late. Miles would be on the doorstep and she'd have to talk with him. That, she couldn't bear; for although she had scarcely seen him, she felt he had been in her life for countless ages. In a rather unreasonable relationship. It was as if all the usual glamour standards were unappreciated by him. He seemed to do his appraising from a different angle—some private yardstick— and she had no inkling as to how she measured up. She thought, we can't go on with this see-saw forever. Even if it meant giving up her share of the dog. If he really loved the puppy, he should have him; at any rate he'd have to prove his love. And if not, then she would take the dog for keeps.

Either way, it would be the end of Miles.

She'd just have to think up a test.

She walked on faster now, small drops of rain glistened on her hair as it flamed in the misty light. Miles, close behind her, watched it lift and fall on her shoulders. Descriptive adjectives crowded in on him. He chose tawny and let the rest go.

And it was when Belinda was within a block of her home that the great idea came to Miles. What one had to do was to put the dog in a perilous position (not too perilous, but perilous enough) and then watch Belinda's reaction. One could immediately deduce the state of her affection. The idea pleased him.

He watched her now, as she approached the crossing, walking faster. Then he saw her lift her head. Obliquely, as she looked toward Victory, he saw how she was smiling—the smile of one who has just recognized an excellent idea.

He quickened his pace, so that he might overtake her, here, by the traffic block.

But Belinda, with head lifted high and a bright smile still on her face, stepped happily off the curb, entirely oblivious that the lights were scarlet against her and that the traffic had the right of way on a wet road.

As the car struck her, she let go of the dog's leash.

There was a nasty moment when all around her were noise and blackness; then sharp streaks of brilliance shot through the dark and she was lying on

157

the sidewalk with her head pillowed on something, and her hair being caressed, while a voice
said, "Are you hurt, Belinda? Belinda, are you
hurt?" And not just any voice: but Miles' voice.

She thought, even while the darkness cleared off,
something is wrong—it shouldn't be me he pets. It
should be the dog. For she remembered the idea
that had come to her: how she would test Miles'
affection, by putting Victory in a dangerous position (but not too dangerous). Then she also re-
called this wasn't part of her scheme. This was
something else. She had presence of mind enough
to keep her eyes closed.

"Darling," he said, "speak to me!"

She fluttered her eyelashes, wondering whether
they were alone. They weren't. A circle of delighted
bystanders gazed down with interest.

She approved of his conversation—an improve-
ment on the one they had when they first met at the
dance. And she let her eyes stay closed.

A heavy voice from the public said, "She don't
look bad to me—"

Belinda's pillow moved smartly, so that she knew
her head had been resting on Miles' knee and
Miles' voice said threateningly, "If you've harmed
one hair of her head—"

The man muttered something about what traffic
lights were for anyway and the atmosphere fresh-
ened. Belinda thought she might soon be flat on the
hard sidewalk, if Miles went physically as well as
mentally to her defense, so she sighed and slowly
opened her eyes.

158

"There, she's coming around," said the man. "Look at her now."

So they all did. Light glinted on the gentian-blue eyes and the flaming hair. She felt no pain, just a vague disappointment that a promising situation had been curtailed so swiftly. Then, suddenly, she didn't like the comic side of it. She wished that the crowd would go and that Miles would take up from where he had left off, quietly and seriously. She felt she knew more about Miles' private standards now.

The man, who seemed to be the driver of the car, said, "Looks as if I can be getting along—"

Miles said, "You can thank your lucky stars—"

There was a faint titter of appreciation from the onlookers, but on the whole they decided the best was past and they might as well go on about their business. Within the thinning circle, Miles helped Belinda to her feet. She brushed herself down as best she could. Miles watched her. Out of her pocket fell the ticket that had won a portion of Victory at the ball. It gleamed up at him—989. Only she hadn't called it that. She'd called it 686. He looked at her standing there, slender and young, with her chin tilted up, setting back her red-gold hair. Quite firmly, Miles put his foot flat across the square of pasteboard: 989 or 686—they'd never really know.

A small boy held Victory on his leash. "This belong to you?" he asked.

Belinda nodded. "Yes," she answered, "It's—"

and was blocked for a want of a word. "Mine," but it wasn't. She hesitated.

"Ours," said Miles.

And somehow they both knew that was the right answer.